How far can Elizabeth run?

"Elizabeth!" she heard someone shout. Through the driving rain she saw Tom Watts charging down the sidewalk toward her.

What is going on? she wondered. *Everywhere I turn today, there he is. And he looks* awful! His scruffy appearance went far beyond someone who'd gotten caught in the rain. He was filthy and unshaven—wild looking, like some deranged vagrant.

"*E-liz-a-beth!*" he bellowed.

He sounded so pathetic, she couldn't help but pause and look back again. *What has happened to him?* she thought with disgust. *Never in my wildest nightmares could I have imagined Tom like this.*

As Tom limped steadily toward her Elizabeth realized that he'd already closed up much of the distance between them. With a gasp she spun around and scurried away. He was beginning to scare her.

"Elizabeth, wait! I have to talk to you!" He leaped from the sidewalk and cut across the muddy lawn.

From the corner of her eye she saw him splashing, slipping, and sliding closer and closer. Horrified, she turned her fast walk into a jog and then into an out-and-out run.

Bantam Books in the Sweet Valley University series.
Ask your bookseller for the books you have missed.

And don't miss these Sweet Valley
University Thriller Editions:

Visit the Official Sweet Valley Web Site on the Internet at:

http://www.sweetvalley.com

SWEET VALLEY UNIVERSITY®

Good-bye, Elizabeth

Written by
Laurie John

Created by
FRANCINE PASCAL

BANTAM BOOKS
NEW YORK · TORONTO · LONDON · SYDNEY · AUCKLAND

RL 8, age 14 and up

GOOD-BYE, ELIZABETH
A Bantam Book / April 1998

ISBN: 0-553-49222-5

Published simultaneously in the United States and Canada

Bantam Books are published by Bantam Books, a division of Bantam
Doubleday Dell Publishing Group, Inc. Its trademark, consisting of the
words "Bantam Books" and the portrayal of a rooster, is Registered in
U.S. Patent and Trademark Office and in other countries. Marca
Registrada. Bantam Books, 1540 Broadway, New York, New York 10036.

PRINTED IN THE UNITED STATES OF AMERICA

OPM   0 9 8 7 6 5 4 3 2 1

To Trudy Carter

Chapter One

"Elizabeth," Tom Watts whispered, looking up into the black starry sky as he stood in the garden behind the Theta Alpha Theta sorority house. "I'd even try wishing on stars if I thought it'd bring us back together again."

And suddenly, magically, she was there beside him. Although her beautiful face was in shadow, her blond hair sparkled golden in the moonlight. Tom let out a sigh of fulfillment as Elizabeth Wakefield slipped into his arms.

His heart felt as if it would burst from happiness as he impatiently began to cover her face with kisses. "I love you, Elizabeth Wakefield," he murmured against her soft cheek. "I have never stopped loving you."

"I love you too, Tom," Elizabeth replied.

And immediately, before she had a chance to take back the words he had longed to hear, he covered her lips with his. . . .

Beep-beep . . . beep-beep . . . beep-beep . . .

"What?" Tom cried as Elizabeth dissolved from his

1

arms. *No. No, no, no. Not the alarm,* his mind screamed. *I don't want to wake up. This dream is too perfect.*

"Elizabeth, come back," he mumbled, burrowing his head deeper into his pillows. Why couldn't a dream be like a videotape he could pause and later come right back to where he left off—or better yet, rewind and replay his favorite moments? Tom would've replayed that kiss about a million times.

But it was too late now. The dream was ruined, and consciousness was flooding through. Elizabeth's face had become Jessica's, and the horrible truth of last night's party at Theta house came back to him in an icy, soul-freezing rush.

Beep-beep . . . beep-beep . . . beep-beep . . .

Groaning, Tom swam out from under the covers and slapped at the insistent alarm clock. It fell to the floor—probably broken, but he didn't care. Not as long as it stopped that infernal beeping.

Sitting up on the edge of the bed, he rubbed his unshaven face and ruffled his hair. Through sleep-blurred eyes he tried to focus on the starkly lit dorm room. The other bed was empty. That was good. He wasn't in the mood to make polite conversation with his roommate, Danny Wyatt, this Saturday morning.

"Why wouldn't you let me sleep just ten more minutes?" he muttered to the offending alarm clock. "Just long enough to convince Elizabeth to forgive me."

Now his beautiful dream had turned into a nightmare that no alarm clock could wake him from—reality. He really *had* kissed Elizabeth in the

2

garden behind Theta house last night. Or he'd *thought* he had. It wasn't until the fifth, or sixth, or seventh kiss that Tom had begun to realize something wasn't quite right. And when he'd tilted her face up to look into those familiar blue-green eyes, he'd discovered that they weren't glittering with love, as he'd hoped, but filled with blank, nervous anxiety.

Confused, he'd cast his glance over her again. Elizabeth's hairstyle . . . Elizabeth's coat . . . but not Elizabeth at all. The realization that he'd just passionately kissed Elizabeth's identical twin sister, Jessica, had swept over him like a chill.

Tom had stood staring at Jessica for what seemed like forever—unable to utter a single word until Jessica herself broke the spell.

"I think Elizabeth saw us, Tom," she whispered. It was the very last thing he'd wanted to hear. Terrified, he'd run inside to find Elizabeth and explain.

"She's gone," Isabella Ricci had said. "She made a speech thanking everyone for the party—and then she ran out of here sobbing." Isabella had then given him a look that left no doubt whom she blamed for Elizabeth's tears.

Had she seen him kissing Jessica too? Probably not. Isabella didn't need new fuel for her disgust. She'd been angry with Tom ever since he and Elizabeth had split. She hadn't exactly *told* him that, though; he'd heard it via her boyfriend, who also happened to be his roommate and best friend.

3

Danny had mentioned several times that Isabella thought Tom was being unfair to Elizabeth. Only in recent weeks did he come to agree with her.

On hearing Isabella's veiled accusation last night, Tom had dashed back to the garden, where Jessica had remained, cowering.

"Jessica!" he'd shouted angrily. "Why were you trying to trick me?"

Instead of answering him, she too had run away in tears.

After that, what else could Tom do but leave as well? His good mood was spoiled. His hopes of reaching Elizabeth were dashed. And he was way too embarrassed and confused to face his friends. It had been a horrible, horrible night—a night he wished he could forget.

How could I have been such a fool? he asked himself. *How could I not know I was kissing Jessica instead of Liz?*

He walked over to the sink and splashed cold water onto his face, hoping to shock the last bit of sleep from his brain. "Get moving, Watts," he told his reflection. "No more wimpy apology letters. This time you've got to face Elizabeth no matter *how* humiliated you are."

As he reached for the phone nervousness made him hesitate, but he pushed it aside. He couldn't afford to waste time because when the semester ended, so did his chances. Elizabeth would be leaving Sweet Valley University forever. Thanks to her slimy new boyfriend, Scott Sinclair, she'd been

4

accepted at the prestigious Denver Center for Investigative Reporting.

I'm happy for you, Elizabeth, if you're happy, he thought as he dialed her number. *But I can't let you leave SVU thinking I made a play for your sister. Please hear me out . . . just this once.*

Suddenly the image of Jessica's anxious, guilt-ridden face swam before him, unbidden. He couldn't even begin to guess what had been going on in her head last night.

Fear clutched at Tom's stomach. *How am I going to explain what happened when I don't understand it myself?*

"Wake up, honey."

Jessica Wakefield yawned and sleepily brushed her tousled blond hair away from her face. The handsome face of her boyfriend, Nick Fox, hovered before her, startling her until she remembered where she was.

"Rise and shine, sleepyhead." Nick flashed her a hundred-watt smile. "I fixed you breakfast in bed."

"Breakfast in *couch,* you mean." She raised herself up on one elbow and rotated her stiff, aching neck.

Nick set a covered tray on the cluttered coffee table in front of her. "OK, breakfast *beside* the couch, if you want to get picky about it." He knelt down and kissed her gently on the forehead. "How'd you sleep?"

"Great," she drawled, not caring if he caught the sarcasm in her voice or not. Nick's couch, cozy enough when she and Nick were cuddling or

watching TV, was *definitely* not made for sleeping. Besides being lumpy, it was half a foot too short for her. She stretched with a groan, wondering if her spine was now permanently curved.

"Beggars can't be choosers," Nick teased.

She whacked him with a pillow. "I hate people who are cheery when they wake up."

"I didn't just wake up. I've been up for hours—"

She snorted in disbelief.

"OK, maybe not hours," he amended, "but I've been up long enough to fix your favorite—banana pancakes." He whipped the white dish towel off the tray, revealing a gargantuan stack of steaming pancakes, a glass of orange juice, a cup of coffee, two slices of bacon, and three yellow flowers in a vase.

Jessica was impressed, even though the vase was a juice glass and she recognized the pansies from the flower box in the lobby of Nick's apartment building.

Nick took her hand and helped her to a sitting position.

"Thanks," she said, leaning closer to the tray.

Nick was right. She shouldn't complain. After all, it had been her idea to crash on his couch. But what choice did she have? After the stupid stunt she'd pulled the night before, she'd been way too embarrassed to go back to the dorm room she shared with her twin sister. Elizabeth was probably livid—and she had every right to be.

Remembering the look on Elizabeth's face when she'd seen her in Tom's arms, Jessica decided

6

she might hide out at Nick's forever.

"Feeling better now?" he asked after she'd taken a bite of pancake.

"No."

"What's wrong? Are the pancakes dry?" Nick asked, sampling them himself. "Taste fine to me."

Jessica sighed. Once again they weren't on the same wavelength. When they had first started dating, they'd been so in tune that they could finish each other's sentences. Lately they hadn't only quit thinking alike; they didn't even speak the same language anymore.

When Jessica had first fallen in love with the dashing, mysterious undercover cop, she'd been taken by his dangerous edge and exciting lifestyle. Unable to resist the temptation, she'd gotten herself involved in a few of his thrilling assignments and even saved his life.

After that, Nick began to change. Suddenly the man who could be as wild and impulsive as she became increasingly more cautious and conservative. Then just days ago Nick announced out of the blue that he'd gotten the crazy idea to take a leave of absence from the force and prepare to go to college. Even though she was still in love with him, Jessica just couldn't handle Nick's sudden transformation from Mr. Excitement to Joe Book Learner. "The food's great," she clarified halfheartedly, "but it's going to take a lot more than a couple of pancakes to make me feel better."

"I can fix more."

"Nick! You know what I mean. I'm talking about last night. I feel positively *mortified*."

"Relax, sweetie. We already talked this through. So what if Tom thought you were Elizabeth? What's the big trauma? It's not the first time you've ever been mistaken for her."

Jessica nodded. *But usually I don't encourage the mistake,* she thought guiltily. She quickly stuffed a bite of pancake into her mouth and watched Nick's eyes to see if he suspected anything.

Nick's emerald green eyes remained calm.

It's not like I lied, she told herself. *I simply left out one teeny fact. I had to. If Nick knew that I tricked Tom into thinking I was Elizabeth, he'd accuse me of . . . well, take your pick!*

Nick reached over and took a piece of bacon from her plate. "Hmmm. If that's not what's bothering you, then what? You can't be upset because Tom gave you a little kiss. I'm not. So forget it."

She blushed and blamed it on the coffee being too hot. "Little kiss" didn't begin to describe what she and Tom had shared. *Maybe I left out two little details,* she added silently.

"What's bothering me," she began, "is . . . is that I'm scared to think what Elizabeth is going to say when I get home."

"Big deal. You and Elizabeth have argued before, and you've always lived through it."

Jessica clamped down on her fork so hard, she bit her tongue. Why did Nick have to make light of everything she said? Just because he didn't *share* her problems didn't mean they didn't *exist*.

"Yes!" she shouted impatiently. "We've fought plenty, but we don't have time for fighting now. Don't you realize Elizabeth is leaving soon? And I *don't* mean across campus to another dorm." Jessica stabbed her fork straight up in the middle of the remaining pancakes and pushed away the tray. "She's going to Denver, in a whole other state—over a thousand miles away. I know, Nick, because I looked it up on a map! I'm being *deserted!*"

"Elizabeth is your sister, Jess, not your mother. You're not being left on someone's doorstep."

"I *feel* like I am. You don't understand, Nick. We've never been separated like this. I'll be all alone. And I *hate* being lonely."

Nick scooted closer and put his arm around her. "You still have me."

She sank into his arms with a resigned sigh and snuggled against him. "I know."

For a moment she forgot her worries. She breathed in his soapy, fresh-out-of-the-shower smell and relaxed as he stroked her hair. Nick's familiar warmth soothed her, but then he had to go and open his big mouth.

"Do you think the mail has come yet?" Nick pulled his wrist closer to check his watch, evidently forgetting that it was the arm he had around Jessica's neck. As her head was scrunched into an uncomfortable stranglehold he muttered, "I think my entrance exam scores might come in today."

Jessica pushed his arm away. She was sick to death of hearing about stupid exam scores. *Thanks for the reminder, Nick,* she fumed silently. *I'd almost forgotten that an alien was inhabiting my boyfriend's body.*

"What's wrong?"

Jessica jumped up from the couch and stomped her foot. "I'm worried that my sister is going to hate me forever, and *you're* worried about some dumb test scores!"

"Elizabeth could never hate you. You know that."

"I kissed *Tom!* Her *ex-boyfriend!*"

"*You* didn't kiss Tom; he kissed you. Remember?"

A flutter of guilt passed through her, but it was quickly pushed aside by her rage at Nick's cluelessness. "So? How do you think *she's* going to feel?"

"I don't know. Why don't you go ask her? I doubt it'll be anywhere near as bad as you think. Elizabeth knows how impetuous you are."

"I'm not impetuous!"

Nick's laughter infuriated her even more than his words.

"Don't you dare laugh at me!" Jessica flopped back on the couch and shot him a withering look.

"Jessica, you're being silly. Go home and talk to Elizabeth, OK? She's not going to be mad. In fact, when you explain the mistake, she'll probably think it's funny."

"Yeah, *right.*" Jessica agreed that she was going to have to face Elizabeth and tell her the truth, but she wasn't as optimistic as Nick about the end results.

10

Elizabeth didn't have much of a sense of humor when it came to Tom Watts.

Dressed in comfortable jeans and an old T-shirt, Elizabeth Wakefield sat cross-legged on the floor beside her desk. In front of her lay a drawer overflowing with papers, news clippings, photos, and assorted mementos of her life at SVU. It amazed her how she could have collected so much stuff in such a short time. If any of her friends had seen the clutter, they wouldn't have believed it. Elizabeth Wakefield, queen of organized neatness, had a messy junk drawer!

It wasn't messy by choice, though. The plain truth was, Elizabeth had avoided cleaning out the drawer for weeks because she knew it would depress her. Inside that jumble lay too many memories she didn't want to dredge up. But as low as she felt just then, deep depression would have been an improvement.

She rubbed her red, swollen eyes and jumped nervously when the phone rang for the umpteenth time that morning.

"Jessica, if that's you, I'm not answering," Elizabeth shouted angrily at the phone. She couldn't believe that after that shameful scene at Theta house, Jessica hadn't even come home last night. In addition to being furious and hurt, Elizabeth had to cope with worrying about where her sister might have spent the night.

The phone continued to ring. She'd shut the answering machine off; she was in no mood to hear

11

any begging, pleading, let-me-explain messages this morning. *"I said I'm not answering!"* The ringing stopped as if the caller had somehow heard the desperation in her voice.

She returned her attention to the junk drawer and sighed. "Get to it. No time like the present to clean out the past." After all, she would be leaving at the end of the semester. There was no sense dragging junk from her old life into her new one.

She scooted the wastebasket closer to her reach. If there was anything she absolutely couldn't part with, she could always box it up and take it to her parents' house before going to Denver. But most of this junk belonged in the trash.

Like this, she thought, unfolding a newspaper clipping. The black-and-white photo showed her with Tom Watts at the Journalism Awards banquet. His dark hair and chiseled good looks still caused her to ache with longing. He had his arm around her, and they were staring lovingly into each other's eyes.

Elizabeth winced. They looked so happy together. But why shouldn't they have? They had been perfectly happy before Tom's long lost biological father, George Conroy, had appeared out of nowhere and destroyed everything.

She laid down the clipping and picked up a snapshot of herself and Tom, hand in hand, in front of Andre's restaurant . . . the place where Mr. Conroy had actually dared to come on to her. She shuddered at the ugly memory and tossed the photo, along with the clipping, into the wastebasket.

Of course her breakup with Tom wasn't entirely Mr. Conroy's fault. Tom could have chosen to believe her when she had told him his father was making a move on her. Instead he'd accused her of jealousy and backstabbing and every other base emotion in the book. Then he'd basically dumped her.

Elizabeth leaned against her desk and took a couple of deep breaths until she was able to push aside her tears. She'd done enough crying last night to last her the rest of the semester.

The next photo she pulled from the drawer was of Todd Wilkins in his basketball jersey. A bittersweet smile came to her lips as she dropped the photo onto the pile of things she wanted to keep.

Todd had been her high-school sweetheart. They'd broken up when they first came to SVU, but eventually they'd worked out their problems and had even gotten back together after Tom broke her heart. It wasn't meant to be, however. They'd parted ways for good when Todd's then-girlfriend, Gin-Yung Suh, fell gravely ill. After Gin-Yung's funeral they'd both realized that they had only been clinging to the past for consolation when their own current relationships had gone sour. But they'd also agreed they'd always be the closest of friends.

And that's what I need right now, she thought. *A close friend. I need to talk to Todd.*

She groped along the desktop until her fingers

closed over the phone. Pulling it down to her lap, she dialed Todd's dorm room.

"Hi." Todd's familiar voice was faintly distorted by his answering machine. *"I'm not here. You know the drill."*

"Todd. It's me, Elizabeth. No message. I just wanted to talk. I sort of need a shoulder, you know?" She paused, wishing she hadn't blurted that out on tape. It hadn't been long since Gin-Yung's death; Todd had enough of his own troubles to cope with. The last thing he needed was for his old girlfriend to be burdening him with hers. "Well," she hurried, "it's nothing important. I'll call back later."

Nothing important, she repeated silently, replacing the phone on her desk. *Only the rest of my life.*

She picked up another photo. It was a group shot of Elizabeth and Tom at a Theta dance with Jessica and her date, Randy Mason. They were seated around a tiny candlelit table with Elizabeth and Jessica side by side in the center of the photo. It too was a happy photo, but looking at it didn't make Elizabeth happy now. As she stared at her sister's smiling face her own image and Randy's seemed to fade out of the picture, leaving only Jessica smiling at Tom Watts. Slowly that image transformed even more, and Jessica was now melting in Tom's arms—just as Elizabeth had seen her the night before. Even after she closed her eyes, she could still see her sister locked in a passionate embrace with the man she loved—*used* to love.

And might have loved again . . .

This time no deep breaths were able to stop the tears. Elizabeth let them fall as more memories preyed on her confused mind.

After they'd both done successful stories on the Verona Springs Country Club scandal, Elizabeth had begun to feel that Tom was softening toward her. Even her friends were suggesting she give him another chance. She shuddered to think how humiliated she might have been if Scott hadn't discovered Tom romancing Jessica in the garden behind Theta house. He'd brought her to witness the disgusting scene with her own eyes!

She knew in her heart that it wasn't Jessica's fault. Her sister would never do something that hurtful to her, not intentionally. Elizabeth was convinced that whatever had happened last night was ultimately Tom's doing.

Why would he do such a thing? she wondered. *Isn't it bad enough that he drives a dagger into my heart every time I see him draped over Dana Upshaw without his having to go after my own twin sister?*

"Like father, like son," she muttered, tossing the photo onto Jessica's desk. Jessica hadn't dated Randy long, but she'd probably want to keep a photo of the two of them together. Or maybe she'd want the picture because Tom was in it—

Whatever, Elizabeth concluded, cutting off the thought. *I don't want it, that's for sure.*

Elizabeth angrily snatched up a card Tom had

given her and threw it into the wastebasket. She rapidly followed it with a dried rose from the first bouquet he'd ever sent her, a letter he'd sent when he was away at a conference in Las Vegas, and a poem he'd written before they'd started dating.

Then she stopped, wiped her tears with the back of her hand, and fished the poem out of the trash. *I can't throw that away,* she thought, unfolding the notebook paper and reading the tender, beautiful words. There were three of those exquisite poems in the drawer. Each one was full of so much love and passion, it broke her heart to know that they were all lies. Slumping against the edge of her bed, she held the paper to her heart and let the tears roll down her cheeks again.

When she was all cried out, she tossed the poems back into the trash. Why keep them? They only filled her with disappointment and pain. Why remind herself of how gullible she'd been? She knew now that true love wasn't real; it existed only in books.

In real life you just concentrate on what matters, she told herself, *like family.* She looked over at Jessica's bed and sighed. *Well,* career *then,* she amended. Her writing and reporting were the two things she'd always been able to count on.

She picked up a copy of the article she'd written about the Verona Springs scandal for the *Sweet Valley Gazette.* Looking at the article filled her with strength and pride. Here was proof she could manage just fine without Tom Watts. "I'll definitely take this with me to Denver," she murmured. It would be a constant reminder of what she could accomplish if she set her mind to it. She was certain that if not for this informative and hard-hitting article, she'd never have been accepted at the Denver Center of Investigative Reporting in the first place.

Elizabeth laid the article aside and reached back into the drawer. *Now* here's *an article with an entirely different slant on the country-club story,* she thought with an amused grin. She unfolded and smoothed out the article from the national magazine *NEWS2US* that had featured her and Scott as two of America's hottest young journalists. The article had somehow made Scott Sinclair sound like a master detective, ace journalist, and superhero all rolled into one. According to *NEWS2US,* Scott had single-handedly solved a murder and saved everyone involved in the investigation—Elizabeth, Jessica, Tom, and Nick—from being drowned in the Verona Springs Reservoir. Even though the article was supposed to be about the two of them, Elizabeth was described as hardly more than a girl flunky to the boy wunderkind. Jessica wasn't even mentioned, and *she* was the one who'd actually escaped from the locked van that was headed for the depths of the reservoir and rescued everyone, Scott included.

When Elizabeth had first seen the article, she'd been steaming until Scott had explained what had happened. It seemed that the female reporter, jealous of Elizabeth's talent and angered by Scott's rejection, had written the story to spite her. Although it was an absurd article, the large, full-color picture of her and Scott was a good one.

She looked at Scott's twinkling blue eyes and perfect smile. He was charming, confident, unselfish, and most of all he *cared* about her. His praise, support, and affection were exactly what she needed at a time when Tom Watts was doing everything in his power to lower her self-esteem.

"So why did you resist me for so long?" Scott's smiling photo seemed to ask her.

"Because of Tom, that's why!" she cried aloud. "Because I couldn't let go. Because I was stupid enough to believe he'd come back to me. But now I know better. After last night—" She clamped her mouth shut, feeling totally foolish for sitting on the floor talking to a picture. But before she laid the photo on top of the items she planned to keep, she had one last question for it. "So why can't you make me forget about Tom?"

Elizabeth shook her head. *Tom is my past,* she reminded herself. *Scott is my future. Scott and DCIR and my career. Nothing else matters.*

She picked up a test paper that she'd saved from World History 101 and tossed it into the trash. From here on out, she would be concentrating totally on journalism. No more history or math or science— nothing except classes relating directly to reporting. *Scott is right,* she thought. *It's pointless to waste my time taking classes I don't need, even if I do enjoy them.*

She unfolded DCIR's colorful brochure and looked at its towering singles apartments. How nice it was going to be to have her own two-room efficiency apartment all to herself. She'd never have to share a cramped dorm room again. She'd even have her own bathroom!

How could I have had any doubts about this place? she wondered. *Pulitzer Prize–winning instructors, state-of-the-art facilities, a reputation as the best journalism school in the country . . . DCIR has it all.*

As her gaze fell on yet another picture of Tom, she winced. *Well, not everything,* she thought. Her fingers involuntarily crumpled the photo. *But that's good! Once Tom Watts is out of my sight, I can forget him and be free of his abuse once and for all.*

She stuffed Tom's picture into the wastebasket, but that didn't seem final enough. With trembling fingers she retrieved Tom's photo and savagely ripped it to shreds.

Oh, good, it's not crowded, Dana Upshaw thought as she slipped into line at the student union cafeteria. She was too late for the regular breakfast menu, but it wasn't nourishment she was after as much as a quick pick-me-up. Too many late nights had left her dragging. *No, the nights are OK,* she amended. *The problem is too many early rehearsals. No one should have to deal with Mahler and Mozart at seven-thirty on a Saturday morning!*

She selected a chocolate-covered doughnut from the rack of pastries and set it on her tray beside her tall cup of coffee. She stopped to grab a handful of sugar and creamer packets. If she got enough sugar and caffeine in her system, she might actually make it through the day.

When she felt a hand on her shoulder, she jumped in surprise, causing coffee to slosh all over her paper napkins. Quickly she moved her doughnut away from the soggy brown mess.

"Maybe you should lay off the coffee if you're that jittery," a calm, melodic voice suggested.

She whirled around to see Elizabeth Wakefield's new boyfriend, Scott Sinclair, staring down at her.

"Where *were* you?" she asked. "I waited outside the music building for twenty minutes."

He tucked a strand of sun-streaked hair behind one ear. "I got tied up."

Dana tilted her head expectantly, waiting for a real explanation, but none came. Without another word Scott plunked a carton of orange juice onto her tray, picked the whole thing up, and took it to the cashier.

Stunned by his lack of manners, Dana didn't say a word as he paid. She just followed him to a table and sat down. Usually when someone flaked on her, she read them the riot act. But right now she didn't want to take a chance. Ever since the party last night, when he'd sent her to the Theta house kitchen just in time to witness her boyfriend's bizarre lip lock with Jessica Wakefield, Dana had been dying to know what was going on in Scott's scheming little mind. Scott had obviously choreographed the whole

20

thing to keep Elizabeth away from Tom. And anyone who could help Dana out in that department got an A-plus and five gold stars in her book.

"Where's Tom this morning?" Scott asked, breaking open the juice carton.

Dana shrugged. "I don't know."

"Don't you think you should keep a closer eye on your boyfriend?" His tone was joking, but his crystalline blue eyes were dead serious.

"I'll see him later, I'm sure." *As if it's any business of yours,* she added mentally.

Scott's lips pursed in disapproval, but they quickly relaxed into a toothpaste commercial smile. "I like you, Dana. I like your style. Take that outfit you're wearing, for instance. Not everybody can get away with wearing tie-dye and a fringed jacket. Not in this decade anyway. You look like you stepped right out of Woodstock—the *first* one, that is."

"Thanks. That's the look I was going for." Dana ran her finger across the top of her chocolate-covered doughnut, licked her finger, and went back for another taste.

Scott captured her hand. "You have beautiful hands. Musician's hands." His touch tickled as he ran his fingertips across her skin. "Few people are blessed with such long delicate fingers. Such strong wrist muscles."

More puzzled than annoyed, she snatched back her hand and picked up her cup. The steaming coffee was still way too hot to drink, so she held it in front of her face, blowing gently over the top. *What's this guy after?* she wondered.

He continued to smile, and Dana smiled back. *He really is attractive,* she thought, *if you like the type—which I* don't. *He evidently thinks he can flatter a rose out of its thorns, but he's not dealing with a hothouse flower here.*

"I've heard you play," he continued. "You're really good. I was telling my friend Anthony the other day that in my opinion, you were the best cellist on campus."

Anthony? Anthony Davidovic? Dana blinked in surprise that Scott would know her favorite professor on a first-name basis.

"He really should give you more solos."

The way Scott was dishing out the compliments would have embarrassed her if she thought for a moment that he was sincere. But there was something fishy about him—something just a little too slick to be true.

She continued watching him over the rim of her cup. *Fascinating,* she thought. *He looks like a stereotypical dull-witted, bleached-blond beach boy, but he's smart. Not smart enough to fool me, of course. But very smart.*

She hadn't always thought so. When she'd first seen him with Elizabeth at Verona Springs, she'd gotten the impression that he was basically a slacker who grabbed the praise while Elizabeth did all the work. Her suspicions seemed to have been confirmed after that article in *NEWS2US* came out.

Man, was Tom hot when he saw that! she recalled.

But after seeing Scott operate at the big bash the night before, Dana had revised her opinion. Scott Sinclair was one sharp dude . . . in a sneaky sort of way.

As much as she hated to admit it, he'd done her a big favor last night. After all, silly Tom just could *not* get his old girlfriend out of his head! Dana shivered, remembering the horror she'd felt when she saw Tom kissing that blond Wakefield twin. She didn't realize it was the wrong one until Scott had dragged the right one into the kitchen to witness the whole enchilada.

The only thing Dana was curious about was how Scott had convinced Jessica to play along with his grand scheme. It didn't make sense that Jessica would double-cross her own twin sister. But why else would she be kissing Tom when she had that dreamy cop for a boyfriend?

Scott's a smooth one, Dana thought admiringly. *As smooth as silk and twice as slippery.*

"Dana, I think you and I could be friends."

"Oh, really?" she interrupted. "I never imagined that we'd have a thing in common."

"We have plenty in common. Trust me."

"What besides Anthony and . . . my doughnut?" she added as he reached over and broke off half of it.

"You know what I mean," he said testily. "Don't play innocent with me. You and I both have a vested interest in making sure Tom Watts stays the hell away from Elizabeth Wakefield."

Yes, we do, Dana thought, but it wasn't something she liked to admit out loud. Besides, something in

23

Scott's self-assured, smug manner made her feel like challenging him. "Why should *you* care what Tom does? You're dating Elizabeth now. Surely you're man enough to keep her occupied full-time."

Scott gave her a look of cold steel. "Of course. And I plan to keep it that way. But you see, *I'm* not the problem here. Tom is. I hate to tell you this, Dana, but I believe Tom's making moves to keep Elizabeth here at SVU."

Dana bristled. "That's ridiculous! Tom is *my* boyfriend. Are you saying that he and Elizabeth—"

"Don't get all riled up. I know Tom is in love with you—*anyone* could see that. But your man isn't perfect. Try not to get offended by what I'm about to say, but . . . well, Tom Watts is basically a very lazy guy."

"Tom's *not*—"

Scott held out his finger to silence her. "Hear me out. This is for your own benefit." He scooted his chair closer to Dana's and began to speak in a confidential tone. "Tom has hated me ever since I convinced Elizabeth to leave the campus TV station. Do you know why? Because it doubled his workload—maybe even tripled it. You wouldn't believe how much of WSVU's business was actually run by Elizabeth."

Dana knew better. As manager of WSVU, Tom worked day and night to see that everything ran smoothly. He reported, edited, wrote stories, filmed broadcasts . . . he did it all. And he loved his work.

"Scott, assuming this is true," Dana said with a scoff, "then why get upset by it? Elizabeth's got a mind of her own. If Tom asks her to stay, all she has to do is say no."

"It's not that easy, I'm afraid. Elizabeth is a brilliant girl, I know, but she's rather . . . *insecure*. Tom still has a lot of influence over her."

Dana lifted her eyebrows. This was getting more bizarre by the minute. If anything, the opposite was true. It was Elizabeth who still dragged Tom's heart around like a puppet on a string. The witch just didn't want to let him go. Elizabeth was spiteful, maybe. Jealous, definitely. But insecure? Dana couldn't see it.

"I've convinced her that she needs to go to school with me in Denver, but I think she's rather intimidated by the caliber of the program. The thought of leaving the familiar to go to the new frightens her. Sometimes I think she'd be content to stay here and splash away in this little puddle of mediocrity forever."

What an elitist snob! Dana thought. *He's got some nerve putting down SVU, especially since it's a known fact that he only got into DCIR because his dad's company funds the undergrad program.* Dana grinned as she recalled how Tom had revealed that little piece of information on a WSVU newscast. If Scott was going to act high and mighty with her, then he deserved to be taken down a peg or two.

"So why are you so anxious to get Elizabeth away from here?" she sneered. "Do you want her to do *your* work?" It made perfect sense. Family connections could get him there, but only Elizabeth's

25

brains could keep him. As much as Dana hated to acknowledge it, everyone knew Elizabeth was a top-notch reporter.

A wicked gleam came into Scott's eyes. "I wish I could say I want Elizabeth to go to Denver because it's the best thing for her career, but I'm not quite that unselfish. Besides, you seem like the type of girl who'd see through me in a minute if I tried to lie. So I don't mind telling you the unvarnished truth. I want Elizabeth to come with me to DCIR because we're meant to be together. You see, I truly love her. I couldn't live without her."

What a crock, Dana thought. *Scott isn't in love with* anyone, *except possibly himself.* He probably considered Elizabeth a trophy girlfriend. She provided the perfect complement to his healthy, blond, tan, outdoorsy look. On the surface they could have been the poster couple for the beaches of southern California.

Scott's chin-length hair fell across his eyes, making them even more shaded and hard to read. "Honestly, Dana. Elizabeth is the perfect woman for me. She has everything—beauty and brains. I simply can't go on to Denver without her. My whole *future* depends on this. I can't let Tom convince her to stay here. That's why I need your help in keeping them apart. Elizabeth *can't* be allowed to see Tom alone . . . not even for a second. Do you understand?"

"I thought you already *had* help."

Scott flipped back his hair and squinted across

the table. "What are you talking about?"

Dana bit her lip. "Maybe I'm wrong, but after that scene between Tom and *Jessica*—"

A slow smile grew across Scott's face, and he laughed heartily. "Wasn't that kiss a stroke of pure genius? But hey—perfect example of what I'm talking about. If not for Jessica, Tom and Elizabeth would have hooked up at that party last night."

"N-No way!" Dana sputtered furiously. "Tom doesn't . . . you're crazy. No way would they have—"

"Oh yes, they would have. Tom wants her. You can trust me on this."

While Dana admitted nothing to Scott, she stopped arguing. Scott was the kind of guy who was so self-absorbed, he would actually believe his own lies. But unfortunately in this case Scott was *right*. It was almost as if he had read Tom's sappy apology letter to Elizabeth, but Dana knew he hadn't. Only Dana had; she'd stolen it off Elizabeth's WSVU desk before *she'd* even had a chance to read it. It had been burning a hole in the lining of Dana's cello case ever since.

Scott gulped down the last of his orange juice and looked at her seriously. "Jessica's done her job. Now I need you to do yours. You've got to keep a close watch on Tom. Stick by him every *second*. Day and night. Don't let him out of your sight. Keep him away from Elizabeth—even if you have to knock him out to do it."

Knock him out? This is not the attitude of a guy in

love, she thought. *Well, whatever. What's it to me? If it means getting Elizabeth Wakefield away from Tom and out of my hair, I'm all for it.*

Dana wiped her hands and mouth with a napkin and pushed her tray to one side of the table. "Scott, if you'll excuse me, I think I'll wander over to Reid Hall and see if Tom's busy."

The tense expression faded from Scott's face, and he grinned from ear to ear. "Partners?" he asked, reaching out to shake her hand.

"Partners," she agreed.

As long as it's to my advantage, she added silently.

Chapter Two

"I'm sorry, Elizabeth," Jessica mumbled as she stuck her key in the door to room 28, Dickenson Hall. She paused, shook her head, and began again. "I'm so totally sorry." *No, that's not right either!* she chided herself.

Ever since she'd left Nick's apartment, Jessica had been practicing what she was going to say to her sister. So far none of her efforts seemed exactly right. Apologies had never been easy for her, but this one seemed twice as hard. This time she was really, really sorry for what she'd done.

Jessica hiked up the sweatpants she'd borrowed from Nick. Even with the drawstring pulled tight, they were baggy. But she didn't dare come home in the dress she'd worn to the party the night before; any unnecessary reminders of last night would *not* help her case. Taking a deep breath like a swimmer about to plunge into icy water, Jessica pushed open the door.

Elizabeth sat hunched over a pile of news clippings and photos with a dazed expression on her face. Jessica waited, but her sister's inevitable barrage of questions didn't come. In fact, Elizabeth didn't even look up.

"Good morning," Jessica called timidly. "You aren't mad at me, are you, Liz?"

Elizabeth didn't move a muscle.

Jessica sucked in a deep breath. She hated being ignored, even when she was in deep trouble. "Elizabeth . . . yoo-hoo, Elizabeth!"

"Oh," Elizabeth said quietly, looking up at last. "So you finally decided to come home."

Here it comes, Jessica thought. *The lecture.* Usually when Elizabeth began nagging, Jessica hunted down her headphones. But this time she simply dropped her head and let her hair hang into her face. She waited, but Elizabeth didn't say another word.

"Listen, Liz . . . I—see, the reason I—"

"Forget it, Jess," her sister murmured. "Whatever excuse you've concocted, I don't want to hear it. Not today."

Biting her quivering bottom lip, Jessica walked over to her own side of the room, shoved aside a stack of fashion magazines, and flopped down on her bed. "How much do you hate me right now?"

Elizabeth didn't answer. She just went back to sorting through the pile of junk in front of her.

"Liz, don't give me the silent treatment. You know I can't stand that."

"I'm not giving you *any* treatment. I'm just busy," Elizabeth said woodenly.

"We need to talk about . . . last night."

"I *said* I'm *busy*."

"I think what I have to say is more important than . . ." Jessica flailed her arms. " . . . whatever it is you're doing."

"Don't you always," Elizabeth snapped. She swallowed loudly and glared at Jessica. Her face was pale and her eyes red. She looked as if she'd been crying all night and all day.

And it's all my fault, Jessica thought miserably. She got up off her bed and approached her sister. "Oh, Liz. Please let me—"

"OK, let me guess." Elizabeth put a finger across her lips and pretended to concentrate. Then she snapped her fingers loudly. "Oh! I know, Jess. You don't want me to go away mad."

I don't want you to go away at all, Jessica thought, but she didn't dare say it, not with the way Elizabeth was glaring at her.

"Fine. I'll make this easy for you. I'm not mad." Elizabeth scrambled to her feet, dropped an armload of stuff into a garbage bag, and twisted the bag shut with a flourish.

"Well, you're certainly not happy."

"That's right," she huffed. "I'm not. I'm absolutely *numb*. So why don't you leave me alone, OK? We can save our little talk for later. I think I'll run this junk down to the trash chute before—"

"*Leave* the trash!" Jessica yanked the garbage bag from her sister and tossed it to her own side of the room. Taking Elizabeth's hand, she led her over to her bed and gently but forcefully pushed her to a sitting position. "You have to listen to me."

Elizabeth struggled to pull away, but Jessica shoved her down again. "Maybe you don't want to hear it," she said before she lost her nerve. "I don't even want to say it, but I can't let you leave thinking Tom and I were . . . well, you know. I wasn't trying to steal your boyfriend."

Elizabeth violently punched a pillow. "You can't steal something that doesn't belong to me, and Tom *doesn't*. Not anymore."

Jessica leaned toward her sister. It nearly killed her to see Elizabeth so upset. "About last night—"

"Tom Watts is the biggest creep in the world!" Elizabeth's pale face turned pink, and she grasped the decorative knob on the bed's headboard so hard it came loose.

Jessica shrank away in surprise at Elizabeth's statement. For a moment she was almost relieved to think her sister was blaming Tom for the kiss. But with the guilt gnawing away at her insides, Jessica had to confess. "You're wrong, Liz. It's not what you think."

"Not what I think? What am I supposed to think? I don't know how he did it, but Tom is disgustingly low to move in on my very own sister."

"It was *my* fault, not Tom's."

Elizabeth stiffened. "What do you mean?" she

asked. Her voice had fallen to a chilly, low timbre.

"I mean . . . *I* went to him in the garden, Liz. I—I wanted to . . ."

Gasping, Elizabeth clutched her chest. Her eyes sparkled with angry tears. "*You* kissed him? Why would you *do* something like that, Jess? Why?" Her breaths were shallow and fast. "You don't even *like* Tom Watts."

Jessica gulped and stared at her feet. "That's what I want to explain. You see, I only did it because I was trying to get you two back together."

"How in the world was your kissing Tom supposed to get him back with me?"

Jessica steeled her courage, knowing the next words from her mouth were going to make Elizabeth the angriest. "I let Tom think I was you."

"You *let* Tom think you were me?"

As proof, Jessica grabbed the shopping bag she'd brought from Nick's. She reached inside it, dug under her party dress, and removed Elizabeth's trench coat. "See, I put this on and—"

Elizabeth let out a squawk of outrage. "You mean you *pretended* to be me! How could you, Jessica?"

Jessica calmly laid the coat on Elizabeth's bed. "I have an explanation."

"Of course you do." Elizabeth rolled the wooden knob angrily between her hands.

"I thought that if I pretended to be you and was nice to Tom—"

"*Nice?* Is *that* what you call it? You were being a

heck of a lot more than *nice* when I saw you."

"That was an accident . . . sort of." Jessica fidgeted in place, took a breath, and plunged ahead. "See, I really think you and Tom want to be together, but you're both too stubborn to admit it. I wanted to find out for sure how he really felt so I could tell you."

"Oh," Elizabeth sneered. "You're playing undercover cop again. How fun!"

Jessica was irritated by her sister's mocking tone, but now was not the time to press it. She could practically see the steam coming out of Elizabeth's ears.

"Well, what did you find out, Agent Double-o-trouble?"

"I found out that Tom really does love you."

Elizabeth groaned. "Yeah, right. Tell me, how did you reach that brilliant deduction?"

"He *told* me."

Without a word Elizabeth scooped up her teddy bear and hugged it to her chest with one hand. She still clutched the broken headboard knob with the other, her knuckles white.

At least that *got through to her,* Jessica thought. If her sister's reaction proved one thing, it was that Jessica had been right all along. Elizabeth still loved Tom too.

"He told you . . . that he still loved me?" Elizabeth asked incredulously.

"Well, actually he said he loved *me,* but he really thought he was talking to *you,* so . . . yes."

Elizabeth smiled. It was a rather sickly smile, but a smile nonetheless.

Whew! Jessica thought, returning the smile with relief. *Maybe Nick was right. All I had to do was explain, and Elizabeth forgave me. Maybe she does have a sense of humor about Tom after all.*

Letting the bear fall to her side, Elizabeth got up from her bed and moved toward Jessica. Closer, closer, she came with that weird smile on her face. Jessica held out her arms for a hug—but instead of a hug Elizabeth heaved the wooden knob she was holding right at Jessica's head.

"How *dare* you manipulate me and Tom like that!" Elizabeth screamed. All the worry, hurt, and confusion that had been stewing inside her finally spewed out in anger.

Jessica recoiled from the knob's near miss. "Are you *crazy?* I told you I was doing it for *you.*"

"Don't do me any more favors, OK?"

"Well, if I don't, who will? You weren't going to do anything about Tom except mope around and cry."

"It's none of your business *what* I do about Tom. If I want to sit around and cry, then I'll sit around and cry."

"Then *sit* around. Cry all you want to, but do it *here.* . . . Don't run away!" Jessica sank down on her bed and stared at her with vulnerable, pleading eyes.

Elizabeth swallowed back an angry retort. She sighed and began to pace up and down the narrow, empty space between their beds. "I'm not running away. I'm going to Denver because it's a brilliant opportunity for me. I might never get another chance like this."

"You might never get another chance with Tom either."

"Tom?" Elizabeth cried, her patience failing. "Why do you keep harping on *Tom* all of a sudden? You never cared about Tom and me when we were dating."

"Of course I did," Jessica declared. "I just didn't talk about it, that's all. There was no reason to. When you and Tom were dating, I didn't have to worry that you'd ever leave . . . *him,* I mean. He really loves you, Liz. You can't leave him!"

"Jessica," Elizabeth moaned. She could see it all clearly now. Jessica was speaking more for herself than for Tom.

"You can't leave. . . ."

Elizabeth felt her insides caving in. How was it that her twin could always do this to her? Jessica was the ultimate master in getting her own way, and now she wanted to keep her from going to Denver. *I have to be strong,* Elizabeth told herself. *I've made my choice. I can't give in.*

Tears began to run down Jessica's face. "You can't leave me, Liz!"

Despite her resolve, Elizabeth felt her heart melting. She sat down beside her sister and wrapped her in a hug. How could she be mad at her sister, knowing that all she did was out of love and desperation? Kissing Tom was just another of

36

Jessica's well-meaning schemes gone wrong. So why did Elizabeth still feel so awful?

"It'll be fine, Jess," she cooed, patting her sister's back gently. "We'll still be as close as ever. We'll talk on the phone every day if you want. You can even come visit me in Denver over breaks. Think of all the possibilities—a whole city full of new cute guys you've never seen."

Jessica clutched her arm. "It won't be the same! I won't know what to do without you around. I'll be so lonely, I won't be able to stand it."

Elizabeth sighed. She knew exactly what it was like to be lonely. No one had ever been as miserable as she'd been during those first weeks of college when Jessica had decided to room with her friend Isabella Ricci. Not having Jessica around every night had seemed positively unnatural. For a moment Elizabeth wondered if she'd have the same feeling when she got to Denver. *Probably,* she admitted. *But we've got to learn to live apart sometime.*

"Don't be mad at me, Liz," Jessica said, loosening her grip long enough to wipe her eyes.

Elizabeth sighed. How many times had she heard those exact same words from Jessica's mouth? About once a day for the last eighteen years, it seemed.

As Elizabeth looked into her sister's blue-green eyes, full of contrition and circled with runny mascara, she was reminded of all the times in high school when Jessica's schemes had gotten them both in trouble—often Elizabeth more than Jessica. And she knew that now, just like every other time, she was about to give in and forgive her twin.

"I don't want you to hate me," Jessica wailed.

"I don't hate you, Jess." Elizabeth wrapped her arms around Jessica's sagging shoulders. "I could never hate you. But I'm not leaving because of you. I'm doing this because it'll be good for my future."

Jessica pulled away and wiped her nose on a nearby satin pajama top. "I know I shouldn't stand in your way, but . . . well, you know me." She smiled feebly. "I had to try."

"You wouldn't be my Jessica if you didn't." Elizabeth smiled in forgiveness. She could never stay mad at her sister for long. Especially not when she'd soon be leaving her. The truth was, she was going to be every bit as lonely without Jessica as her sister was going to be without her. Sometimes she felt as if they were two halves of the same person.

Be strong, Elizabeth told herself. *Jessica is already convinced you're unhappy about this move. If you break down now, she's never going to give up.*

As Jessica's sniffs subsided, Elizabeth made a show of looking at her watch. "Oh . . . it's getting late," she said, trying to keep the hoarseness out of her voice. "I've really got to run. There's some business I need to take care of at the *Gazette* before my twelve o'clock study seminar. We'll talk later, OK?"

"OK. Better take your umbrella. It looks awful out there."

38

That was a switch—Jessica giving *her* advice—but Elizabeth tried not to dwell on it as she picked up her large striped umbrella and leather backpack and hurried out the door. She'd held in her emotions as long as she could, and there was no way she'd be able to make it down to the lobby in one piece, let alone across campus.

With a shuddering breath she quickly ducked into the ladies' room, bursting into tears before the stall door shut behind her.

The sky was dark and threatening, and the wind was just beginning to whip the treetops as Tom ran toward Dickenson Hall. It seemed almost appropriate that the weather should mirror the storm of emotions that were churning inside him. Tom was feeling it all: dark, stormy, threatened, angry, unsure, but at the moment mostly frustrated. He'd called and called Elizabeth's room, but she wasn't answering the phone. Her answering machine wasn't even picking up.

But I know she's there, he assured himself. *She's got to be. I've looked everywhere else I can think of.*

He blinked in surprise as a drop of rain smacked him in the face. Then another and another. Drops splattered on the dry sidewalk around him. Suddenly, as if someone opened the floodgates, it began to pour. But the modern, multistoried dorm was now in sight, so Tom kept running.

Please be home, Elizabeth, he pleaded silently.

We have to settle this thing once and for all.

Just as he started across the huge parking lot at the rear of the dorm, his heart sank when Dana Upshaw suddenly scurried into view. How could anyone *not* notice her? She was dressed in an orange tube top, a psychedelic miniskirt, a buckskin jacket with insanely long fringe, and knee-high boots that looked as if she'd stolen them off a drunken pole climber. Her long, curly, mahogany hair was up in little-girlish, dog-ear pigtails with a giant orange bow tied around each one. The bows were already starting to droop from the rain.

What on earth is Dana doing standing outside Dickenson Hall . . . in the rain . . . with no umbrella? He ducked his head, hoping she hadn't seen him. But the way his luck was going, he wasn't the least bit surprised to see that she was cutting across the parking lot and heading straight for him like a fringed torpedo.

"Hi, sweetie!" she cried, running up to his side. She shielded her eyes from the rain with one hand as she looked up into his face. "Out for a jog?"

"Something like that. But what . . . what are you *doing* here, Dana?"

"Oh, nothing," she said with a shrug that forced her to readjust her tube top. "I was on my way home from my morning rehearsal and thought I saw you headed this way."

Tom didn't believe her for a second. The music building was clear across campus from Dickenson Hall. Besides, she lived miles off campus. There was no way she just happened to be in the neighborhood.

"How about driving me home?" she asked, wrapping her arm around his waist.

The pressure of her arm pressed his clammy, wet shirt against his back. He gasped and unwound her arm from around his waist. "I don't have time right now."

"You look like you didn't have time to shave or dress properly either. Don't you sleep in those sweats?"

"I'm running an important errand. And you're right, I'm in a major hurry." He stepped to one side, but so did she. "Dana!"

"Well, can't I come with you?"

He shook his head in a frustrated no.

"Errands are always more fun when you have someone along to keep you company," she said.

Tom sighed loudly. "I'd better take care of my business alone, Dana. I don't want you to have to tromp around in the rain."

"I don't mind. In fact, I kind of like it." She grabbed his hand and swung it. "It's romantic."

"Not to me. Sorry, but I really have to go." Again Tom untangled his fingers from hers and stepped to one side, but Dana hopped playfully in his way. They seemed to be doing some kind of crazy dance out on the sidewalk.

"Dana!" Tom scolded.

She giggled and stepped aside, but before he had taken two steps, she was underfoot again. She reminded him of a cat his sister once had that would meet him at the doorway when he got home from school and walk beneath his feet all the way to the kitchen, tripping him every other step.

"You're sexy when you're aggravated," she flirted.

Groaning, he tried again and again to pass her, but she wouldn't stop bouncing into his path.

"Dana, stop it!" he shouted.

Dana froze in place and pouted.

Maybe she's just fidgeting in the rain, Tom thought guiltily. *But why can't she quit jumping around like this is some kind of game?*

Tom had loved Dana's exuberance and energy when they'd first started dating, but lately her bouncy effervescence did nothing but annoy him. When she began blathering about Mahler, Tom had to stuff his hands into his pockets to control his impulse to literally lift her up out of his way and toss her into the nearest puddle.

"Dana, I'm *drowning* here," he whined, wringing water from his sweatshirt.

"Poor baby. We *are* getting soaked. Why don't we go over to the coffee shop? We could grab one of those cozy back booths and cuddle over a cup of hot chocolate instead of standing out here in this downpour like a couple of ducks."

I wouldn't be *standing here if you weren't blocking my way to that door like a psychedelic linebacker,* he thought.

For a moment Tom feared Dana must have read

42

his mind and decided to tackle him for real because she suddenly grabbed him, pulled his face to hers, and kissed him long and hard on the lips.

I don't have time for all this wallowing in self-pity, Elizabeth scolded herself as she paused in Dickenson Hall's glass-fronted lobby long enough to take the cover off her umbrella. She gazed dismally out at the rain and then glanced at her watch. That silly little crying jag in the bathroom had wasted ten minutes. Now she'd barely have time to stop by the *Gazette* before her art history study seminar.

"Hey, Wakefield!"

Elizabeth looked back to see Tonya Teff, a girl from her floor, working behind the front desk. When they'd first met, Tonya hadn't been able to tell Elizabeth and Jessica apart. She'd solved the problem by calling both of them "Wakefield." Even though she'd eventually learned to distinguish be-tween the twins, she still clung to her habit.

"Hope you have your umbrella," Tonya yelled.

Elizabeth pasted a smile on her face and lifted her hand. "I have it right here," she called back.

"You're smarter than those guys," Tonya said with a laugh. "Just look at them out there."

Elizabeth halfheartedly obeyed, looking out the wide glass doors at the many unlucky students who'd been caught by the rain. Some scurried toward the dorm with books over their heads, some danced around like playful children in a sprinkler, and some just stood around like sodden statues. More concerned with her own problems than with the discomfort of her faceless fellow students, Elizabeth slung her heavy backpack over both shoulders to keep her hands free and popped open her umbrella.

"Well, have fun out there," Tonya teased before going back to sorting mail.

With a mumbled good-bye Elizabeth threw her hip against the push bar that opened the wide glass door and stepped outside.

The icy rain wasn't what caused her to gasp. Right in her line of vision stood Tom with Dana wrapped around him like red stripes around a candy cane.

Elizabeth didn't know who to be mad at first: Jessica for feeding her that line about Tom still loving her, herself for believing it, or Tom.

She chose Tom.

How dare he! she thought, seething. *There are a million and one places on this campus where they could go to make out, but no, he has to do it right outside my* dorm!

Elizabeth ducked behind her umbrella as the tears threatened to fall once again. *It's a strange thing about tears,* she thought. *Once they get started, they never seem to want to stop.* This time she didn't bother to wipe them away. Thanks to the rain, no one would notice a little moisture on her cheeks.

He does this on purpose, she mused, using her umbrella to block the ugly scene from her sight as she hurried away. *Why else would he bring Dana all the way over here? Time after time he goes out of his way to hurt me. And every time I let it get to me. Will I ever learn?*

Elizabeth's fingers cramped around the umbrella handle. For a moment, when Jessica had told her that Tom still loved her, she'd let her hopes soar high. Once again they'd been dashed to the ground and stomped on.

It was nothing but a lie, she thought angrily. But she was more angry at herself for believing it than at Jessica for telling it. *She didn't mean to hurt me,* Elizabeth reminded herself.

"But you *did* hurt me, Jess," she muttered, the pounding rain drowning out the sound of her voice. "You shouldn't give me false hope. Tom doesn't love me. And judging from the way he treats me now, I doubt he ever did."

Tom broke away from Dana and sucked in a slow, deep breath. Then, as gently as his lack of patience would allow, he placed both hands on Dana's shoulders, looked deep into her hazel eyes, and spoke as calmly as he could manage. "Dana, if you don't get out of my way *now*, I'm going to walk right over you!"

Unexpectedly a lump formed in Tom's throat as Dana blinked up at him. Little raindrops clung to her dark lashes like tears. She looked devastated. Once again he'd hurt her feelings.

Guilt churned in his stomach. It seemed as if all he did anymore was hurt people. Everywhere he went, he left a wake of crying women: Elizabeth,

45

Jessica, and now Dana. He hadn't meant to hurt her. But why couldn't she see that he wasn't in the mood for her games? Why wouldn't she just go away and leave him alone?

She began to wail. "How can you . . . *sniff* . . . be so mean . . . *sniff* . . . after I saw you kissing . . . *sniff-sniff* . . . *her* last night!"

Her words stopped him cold. "What did you see?"

"I saw . . . *sniff* . . . you, Tom . . . behind Theta house." Dana turned off the sniffing and began to scold in earnest. "Imagine how it made me feel. You were supposed to be *my* date, and there you were kissing Elizabeth Wakefield like there was no tomorrow!" She wiped the rain and tears from her face and lowered her head. "I wasn't just heartbroken, Tom, I was totally *humiliated*."

Tom hung his head guiltily. He couldn't look her in the eyes. "Why didn't you say something?"

"What was I supposed to say? Better yet, *when* would I have had the chance to say *anything*? You dashed off into the night not saying a word to anyone."

"I'm sorry, Dana. I was so upset, I couldn't think straight."

"Apparently not." She put her hands on her hips and glared at him.

"Look, it wasn't Elizabeth, OK? It was Jessica. But I thought—" He stopped short, realizing that this explanation wasn't going to make Dana any happier.

"You just left me at the party like an old raincoat you didn't want," she whined. "I was totally stranded. I had to ask Danny and Isabella to give me a ride home."

"I'm sorry. I—"

"Forget it! It's too late to apologize now!" she shouted. Without another word Dana turned and splashed away across the parking lot.

Well, she's gone, his conscience nagged. *You got what you wanted. Are you happy now?*

Tom hung his head in the rain and sighed. He wasn't happy. In fact, he was truly ashamed. His relationship with Elizabeth had nothing to do with Dana. But somehow, ever since he and Dana had started dating, he'd always allowed Elizabeth to come between them. No wonder Dana was always trying to get his attention; his mind was forever set on his ex-girlfriend. He'd hurt Dana that way countless times, and he'd just hurt her that way again.

Tom looked in the direction Dana had run and considered chasing after her, but it was a very fleeting thought. He couldn't help the way he felt, after all. It was true: He loved Elizabeth more than anything.

His path clear and his sense of purpose restored, Tom ran for the glass doors of Dickenson Hall.

Dana ducked into the three-sided bus shelter and plopped down on the empty bench. She brushed the rain from her face with her hand and squeezed water from her pigtails. Leaning back against the bench, she began to giggle.

"Mission accomplished! Dana, one. Tom, zero."

With a finger she wrote the figures on an invisible scoreboard in the air.

She peeked around the side of the shelter, still grinning. "I know all about your errand, Mr. Tom Watts. And you are too late this round."

Seconds after she'd kissed Tom, she'd seen a familiar blonde scurrying away from the dorm, cowering behind a big striped umbrella. She hadn't been able to see the face clearly, but judging from the size of the backpack, she'd bet her cello it wasn't Jessica. Besides, a woman like Jessica would *never* wear her backpack over both shoulders.

"You won't find your sweet Elizabeth this time, Tom. She's already gone. And what's more, she saw you kissing *me*."

Dana pulled the orange ribbons from her pigtails and shook loose her dark, wet curls. She didn't particularly like tricking Tom, but if she hoped to help Scott with his plan, she'd have to be ruthless. She almost wished that Scott had been around to see her fabulous performance.

"This is even easier than I thought." She laughed out loud and patted herself on the back. "Dana, you're quite the little spy."

As the rain pounded even harder she settled sideways on the bench so she could keep an eye on the door of Dickenson Hall. No doubt Tom would come out very, very soon, and she had to be ready to move.

Chapter Three

_____

"What do you mean, she's gone?" Tom shouted, banging his fists on the reception desk in the lobby of Dickenson Hall. Students turned and looked up from lounge chairs where they huddled with books and soft drinks and bags of chips, but Tom didn't care. He felt he was about to burst with rage and frustration. "Did Elizabeth tell you to say that?"

Tonya Teff stood behind the waist-high reception desk and stared at Tom with wide, startled eyes.

"N-No, T-Tom," she stammered. "When I saw you rush in, I figured you were here to see her. I was just trying to save you the trip. I mean, she went out the door, like, a minute ago. I'm surprised you didn't bump into her."

Tom whirled around to face the doors, sending splatters of water over Tonya and the desk.

"If you hurry, you might be able to catch her," Tonya added. "She's carrying a black-and-white-striped umbrella."

Without so much as a thank-you, Tom furiously dashed back out into the storm. The rain seemed to be coming down harder now, beating against his shoulders and back as if the weather were as angry as he was.

Which way did she go? he wondered, a sense of desolation washing over him. He could hardly see through the gray curtain of driving rain.

"Elizabeth, where are you?" he called.

Shielding his eyes, he peered across the drenched campus. For a second he thought he caught a glimpse of a blond ponytail bobbing ahead beneath a large striped umbrella. Was his luck finally changing?

His heart rate sped up along with his pace. Water squished noisily in his shoes as he ran along the flooded sidewalk. Blinded by the rain and his own single-minded goal, Tom stumbled off the edge. Pain shot up from his twisted ankle as he teetered off-balance and fell into a huge puddle that lay over a newly planted flower bed. He gasped as his hands and knees sank into the soft mud.

Ignoring the pain in his ankle, he hobbled to his feet. Quickly he reached up to wipe the rain from his eyes but only succeeded in wiping a broad smear of mud across his face.

"Elizabeth!" he yelled. But she was nowhere to be seen. He'd lost her again—maybe this time for good. Anguished, he dropped back into the muddy puddle.

He beat the ground with his fists, sending splatters of filthy water in all directions. *"E-liz-a-beth!"* he cried helplessly, his voice swallowed up by the pounding rain.

When Elizabeth arrived at the *Gazette* offices, she was slightly disappointed to find Scott busily shuffling through their desk drawers. Any other time she would have been glad to see him, but she had a story to proofread and was rushed for time. Besides, she knew her face was puffy from crying, and she didn't want him to see her so upset.

"Elizabeth! I've been so worried about you," he said. He pulled out a file folder, slammed the drawer shut, and rushed around the desk to meet her. "How are you this morning?"

"Fine," she said mechanically.

"I would have called, but I wanted to let you sleep late today. I figured as upset as you were, you might've had trouble falling asleep last night."

Well, at least someone *is concerned about me,* she thought. She relaxed and even felt a smile begin to creep across her face. *Why shouldn't I smile?* she asked herself. *It's refreshing how Scott puts my needs ahead of his own.*

Scott returned her smile and reached out for her hand. The warmth of his touch took away the chill of the rain.

How could I ever have doubted his motives? she wondered. *He's been so supportive. Anyone could see that he only cares about what's good for me.*

"I still can't believe the way Watts was carrying on with Jessica at your party last night." He shook his head. "What a pig! What you ever saw in that creep beats me."

Elizabeth's fleeting smile evaporated as quickly as it had begun.

"Oh, sorry." Scott's face reddened. "I know you must be pretty upset. I wish there was something I could do to make you feel better."

His obvious discomfort made Elizabeth feel guilty for dragging him into her bad mood. "Well, I could use a hug," she said, holding open her arms.

As Scott wrapped his strong arms around her Elizabeth's original idea of a friendly, forgive-me-for-being-grumpy hug changed. Suddenly she needed to be held, protected. She longed to lose herself and her problems in his embrace.

Scott moaned softly as she pulled him closer. "Is there anything else I can do for you?"

"I suppose I could also use a little kiss."

Scott eagerly brought his lips to hers. Elizabeth clung to him and returned his kiss hungrily, still looking for that moment of escape. Briefly she thought she'd found it.

"Is that what you had in mind?" he asked when they broke apart.

"Exactly what the doctor ordered," she said, touching a fingertip to her lips.

Scott swept himself into an exaggerated courtly

bow. "Is there anything else I can do for you, milady? Your wish is my command."

"No. What I'd *really* like even *you* can't provide for me, Scott."

"Try me. I'm a pretty resourceful guy." Taking both her hands in his, he leaned back against the desk. "Your wish is my command."

"I wish . . . I could get away from this place."

"From the office? That shouldn't be a problem." Dropping her hands, he stuffed the file folder into his briefcase and snapped it shut. "I'm finished here. You want to go for a cup of coffee?"

"No, I meant I wanted to get away from this *campus*. I'm so sick and tired of . . . you know. Everything!"

"I know what you mean. I'd like to get away from it all too—well, almost all." He pulled her back into his arms. "Not you. I don't want to be away from you for a minute. I'd only leave here if I could take you with me." He tenderly brushed a strand of hair from her face and laid his hand against her cheek. "I'm not one of those things you want to run away from, am I?"

"No," she said with a sigh. "But—"

"Then let's do it!"

"Do what?"

"Leave."

"Very funny," she said, pulling away. For a moment he'd seemed so sincere. Now he was just making fun of her.

"I mean it." He held his palms upward.

"What's stopping us from going to Denver early? There's no law that says we have to wait for the semester to end. Let's go now."

"We can't."

"Of *course* we can. We've already put deposits on our rooms. Two perfectly good suites are just sitting there empty. Why wait? We could use the extra time to get settled in. See Denver. Make some connections. It'd be a great opportunity for us to get a jump on things."

"What about the little matter of our classes here?"

"What about them? Honestly, Liz." He poked her backpack with his foot. "It's a *Saturday*, for goodness sake. Who cares about a study seminar? Besides, what's art history going to do for you besides develop your muscles from carrying that twenty-pound book around? Your goal in life isn't to work in some stuffy museum. You're going to be an investigative reporter. So forget SVU, already."

"But if we quit now, we'll fail. I can't—"

"What do you think employers look at, Liz? Grades or experience?"

"I can't just quit!"

"Well, we can apply for an emergency leave. Take incompletes or something. Believe me, if you know the right people, it can be worked out."

Elizabeth looked at him doubtfully but quit protesting. Scott always seemed to have an easy answer. No rules ever slowed him. No fence ever seemed to stop him. Worry was evidently not a part of his vocabulary. But was that necessarily a bad thing? She was known to have a bit of a stubborn streak herself when it came to doing something that she really felt was right.

Maybe I should try to be more like Scott, she thought. *More spontaneous, less cautious.*

"We can leave anytime. Even tomorrow, if you want." He chuckled, but his blue eyes were dead serious.

He apparently mistook her hesitation for agreement. "All righty, then." He held up his briefcase. "I'll finish up this last story and start making our travel arrangements right away."

"Whoa, back up the train a moment." Despite her recent resolve to be more spontaneous, Elizabeth didn't want to go overboard. There was a big difference between spontaneity and recklessness. She took a step backward. "I was just fantasizing earlier. Leaving tomorrow is not really what I'd call a practical suggestion."

"Of course it is, if you want it to be."

Elizabeth's eyes widened in amazement. "I don't *want* it to be! Not really anyway. I was just talking."

Scott shook his head sympathetically. "I think you're kidding yourself, but OK." He tucked his hair behind his ears. "I'll go along with whatever you say. I know how you are. You wouldn't think something was worthwhile unless you could panic and worry about it first."

55

She glanced at her watch. Her seminar was starting up soon, and she didn't have time to get into a deep, future-affecting discussion.

Scott draped his arm across her shoulders. "Elizabeth, you may or may not have been serious, but I am. I want you to know that I'm here for you. Your options are always open. Anytime you decide things aren't worth it around here and you want to leave, you just call, and I'll be happy to drop whatever I'm doing and head east with you."

Elizabeth smiled. "Thanks. But I think we'd better stay and face the music a while longer."

"It's your decision. But hey, as long as we're here, there's a big party at the Patmans' tonight. I know it's short notice, but how'd you like to go?"

"I didn't know you knew the Patmans."

He laughed. "There are a lot of things you don't know about me yet, Miss Wakefield. But yes, I know the Patmans. My dad and Bruce's dad are friends from way back." He picked up his briefcase and slung his jacket over his shoulder. "Well, what do you think? Wanna go hobnob with the rich?"

A party at the Patmans' sounded awfully inviting. It would be a perfect way to get her mind off her troubles. And besides, that would be one place in Sweet Valley where she could be sure *not* to run into Tom Watts. "I'd love to," she replied.

"Great. I'll call you later with the details. Bruce said it's informal, but wear something professional looking. There are going to be some pretty influential people there I want to introduce you to. How about that white suit of yours?"

"OK," Elizabeth said. She couldn't remember the last time a date made a wardrobe request, but it seemed a simple enough favor to ask, if the suit was clean. She hoped Jessica hadn't borrowed it.

Scott grinned. "Now that that's all settled, is there anything else I can do for you?"

"How about another kiss?"

"Gladly." Scott dropped his briefcase and jacket to the floor and pulled Elizabeth into his arms.

Denise Waters stood nervously behind her boyfriend, Winston Egbert, as he rang the doorbell outside the massive oak front door of the Patman mansion.

"That's Morris, the butler," Winston whispered as a tall, thin, elderly man answered the door.

"Mr. Egbert, Miss Waters," Morris said emotionlessly. He swung the door wide and gestured for them to enter the Patmans' elegant foyer. "Mrs. Patman said you'd be arriving this morning." Denise stood very still and tried not to drip on the gleaming tile floor. *What a time for rain!* she thought.

Morris lifted one eyebrow slightly. It was the closest his face came to registering any disapproval.

Denise quickly leaned toward Winston's ear and whispered, "See. I *told* you we were supposed to use the back entrance."

"And I told you, I've known Bruce since kindergarten," Winston hissed back. "I don't have to skulk around to the servants' entrance."

"Why not? Today that's exactly what we are. We're the caterers, remember?"

Winston flicked her away and turned back to Morris. "Can we get some help unloading all this food for the dinner party?"

The elderly butler pursed his lips, then glanced out the front door. "And your van is where, exactly?"

"My *van* is right there." Winston pointed to the orange Volkswagen Bug that sat in the driveway.

Morris cleared his throat.

"OK," Winston conceded. "It's not your typical caterer's van, but it's the closest thing I've got. And all the food fit in it without a hitch," he added with a hint of defensive pride in his voice.

Morris held open the door again, this time gesturing for them to go back outside. "Mr. Egbert, if you'll follow the drive to the left, it'll take you around to the back of the house. It will be much more convenient to carry the food to the preparation area from there, and the covered walkway will keep you and the food out of the rain. I'll have Evangelina waiting at the kitchen entrance to give you whatever assistance you might require."

As they dashed back out to the car Denise couldn't resist a little dig. "I told you so," she sang.

Winston pretended to ignore her. He just started the VW and drove around the curving drive, muttering under his breath all the while.

As promised, Evangelina met them around back.

She let them inside, showed them around, and then disappeared back to her own duties.

"Looks like the servants' entrance to me," Denise teased again as they carried in the last load of sacks and boxes. Dropping her load on the kitchen island, she laughed and leaned playfully against him. "Don't make such a face, Winnie. We should make enough from this dinner to get me out of debt, and you'll never have to use the servants' entrance again."

"Until the next time you go credit card crazy."

Denise winced at the painful reminder. "Never!" she vowed, drawing an *X* across her heart. "I've learned my lesson. Once I get these bill collectors off my back, I swear, no credit cards for this girl ever again."

Denise still couldn't believe how she'd let herself get so deeply in debt. She was usually such a responsible, practical person. But the moment she'd gotten that first plastic card in her hand, she'd gone wild. It'd been so easy. See it? Like it? Then charge it, and it's yours. It'd been fun too—until it'd all snowballed into an avalanche of debts. Before long she was borrowing from one credit card to pay another. Now she was in big, big trouble. This catering job for the Patmans was her last chance to get out of debt.

"I certainly hope you've learned your lesson!" he said as he unloaded the contents of a cardboard box into the refrigerator.

"Don't you get uppity with me, Winston Egbert. Half of that stuff I bought was for *you*, you know."

"I know. And I'm paying for it. Dare I list all the indispensable services I provide completely gratis? VW driver, box toter, grocery buyer, plate washer, spoon licker—"

"Lobster spoiler."

Winston put on a pained expression and pretended to pull an arrow from his wounded heart. "Look at it this way," he said when he'd recovered from his imaginary stab wound. "If I hadn't left those lobsters in the trunk of my car, we'd never have created lobster *al* Denise for Elizabeth's party."

"*You* created lobster *al* Denise," she reminded him. "I prefer to call it Winston's tofu wonder."

"Because it's *wonder*-ful?"

"Because people are going to *wonder* where the lobster went."

Winston rolled his eyes dramatically. "OK. I created it. And if I hadn't, Bruce would never have tasted it, never have fallen in love with it, and never have hired us to cater his parents' dinner party. So the way I figure it, you really owe me big time, Denise."

"Really? Is that so?"

"Sure. Anybody can cook plain ol' lobster, but no one except the two of us knows the secret lobster *al* Denise recipe."

"Let's hope they never find out." Denise's heart fluttered nervously at the very thought.

"It's going to work out fine, you'll see. Even better than we'd originally planned. We hardly broke even after buying all that stuff to cater last night's party. But with this gig you're going to be out of debt pronto. How could we miss? They pay for lobster, and we pay for tofu. Do you know how cheap that stuff is?" Winston laughed uproariously.

"Seriously, Winnie. I'm worried about tonight. It's one thing to serve a bunch of college kids paprika-covered tofu and tell them it's lobster, especially when you're in a pinch and don't have a choice. But these are adults. Really *rich* adults. Mr. and Mrs. Patman are going to know the difference."

"Bruce and Lila didn't."

"Well, that may be one of the great mysteries of the universe. I don't know why they didn't realize the lobster was fake. Especially Bruce, the way he brags about being a seafood connoisseur and all."

"You know Bruce. He's mostly a lot of hot air. If he's not bragging, he's asleep."

"But his parents will know—"

"No more worrying." Winston held out his hand like a cop halting traffic. "We have work to do." He handed Denise one of the Patmans' silver serving trays. "Time to artfully arrange the hors d'oeuvres."

Dutifully she began transferring stuffed mushroom crowns and cream-cheese puffs from the plastic containers she'd filled at Theta house to the trays. "Wouldn't it be great to have a place like this?" she asked, looking around at the sumptuous kitchen in awe.

"Don't get any ideas. You're not out of the woods yet."

"I'm not buying. I'm just *imagining*." She ran

her hand along the smooth marble countertop and down the side of the cabinet. "Look at this wood. Most people I know don't have *furniture* this nice."

"Too much stuff, if you ask me," Winston said. "Why would one family need two of everything? Two refrigerators. Two ovens. Two sinks."

"I'll bet all these pots and pans hanging around cost more than my college tuition. And look at the spices! You'd think the Patmans were gourmet cooks."

"They aren't, but I'm sure they probably have one—no, make that *two* gourmet cooks on salary."

"I'm sure they do. And probably either one of them could have prepared the food for this dinner party. We were really lucky to get this job."

Winston nuzzled Denise's neck. "Someday I'll buy you a kitchen like this," he promised.

"Oh, right. I can just see us now." Denise stuck her nose high into the air. "Winnie, deah," she said in a feigned genteel voice. "Did you give the maids the night off?" She tiptoed her fingers across the counter and up his arm.

"Yes, dah-link. I dismissed all fifteen of them. We're all alone tonight."

"Whatever are we to do?" She snapped her fingers. "I know, let's cook our own meal! Wouldn't that be jolly fun? We can experiment in our very own kitchen." She looked around as if lost. "Where do you think Evangelina finds the *food?*"

"I'm sure it's around here somewhere, but what shall we make that won't get our delicate fingers smudged?" Winston asked, wriggling his fingers in front of Denise's face.

She laughed, shedding her fake identity. "You? Nothing! You could make a mess cooking a TV dinner."

"TV dinner? What's that?" Winston sniffed, letting her know that the game wasn't over.

"Sorry, deah." She placed the back of her hand against her forehead in a dramatic pose and resumed her nasal voice. "Oh, pumpkin, look! The trash can is positively overflowing!"

"Then we *simply* must buy a new one," Winston clowned, reaching for his wallet.

"Oh yes, let's. Why don't we purchase a silver one this time?"

"You know how Evangelina hates to polish the silver."

"Then how about a gold one!"

"Yes. Gold," Winston agreed. "What a divine idea. My dah-link, have I ever told you you're a woman of discriminating tastes?"

"You think so?"

Winston swept her into his arms. "Of course. Why else would you have chosen me?" He tilted her backward and began to cover her exposed neck with kisses.

Giggling, Denise went limp in his arms. Her head fell farther back until her chestnut-colored hair raked the floor. Winston stumbled, nearly dropping her, but he regained his balance and resumed his noisy kissing.

From this nearly upside-down position Denise saw the swinging door open. Her gaze went from the expensive leather shoes to the soft silk slacks on up to the perfectly composed face of Bruce's mother, Marie Patman.

Denise coughed, stumbled upright, and jumped away from Winston. Her face, red from dangling upside down, got even redder with embarrassment.

"Mrs. P-Patman," she stammered. "Hello." She elbowed Winston discreetly, urging him to wipe the silly expression off his face. Mrs. Patman's serene face gave no indication that she'd seen Winston and Denise clowning around. "You must be Bruce's friends," she said, holding out her frail hand. "Welcome to our home. I hope you've been able to find whatever serving dishes you need."

"Yes, ma'am." Denise gulped. "Evangelina had everything laid out for us."

"Yes, Lina is a wonder. She's been with us for years." Mrs. Patman leaned confidentially toward Denise. "Henry is right behind me, so I'll be brief. I wanted to make certain you remembered the poppy seed dressing we asked for. I hate to be a bother, but Henry will eat nothing else on his salad."

Denise smiled politely. "Of course we have it. While I was preparing what I could at Theta house, Winston did the last minute shopping. . . ." She trailed off when she caught a glimpse of her boyfriend. *What is he doing now?* she wondered distractedly.

Winston was jumping up and down behind Mrs.

Patman's back, waving his arms and shaking his head like he was playing some crazed game of charades. *Oh, great,* she thought. *Winston forgot the salad dressing. What a surprise!*

"Oh, here you are, Marie." Dressed in tennis whites, Henry Patman strode through the door. It was easy to see what Bruce would look like someday. Mr. Patman shared the same finely chiseled jaw and boyish handsomeness that his son was famous for. He had Bruce's glittering blue eyes and dark hair, although Mr. Patman's had just a touch of gray at the temples.

"Winston," Mr. Patman boomed as he slapped Winston on the back. "Good to see you again." He turned and scooped up Denise's hand in more of a hand *hug* than a handshake. "I'm so looking forward to your famous lobster *al* Denise. Bruce has been raving about it all day."

"Yes, my dear. We've heard so much about your skill with seafood," Mrs. Patman concurred. "Henry is an absolute lobster fanatic. I do hope it's not going to be served in the shell, though. Cracking the things can be such a nuisance."

"And messy!" Winston added. "But don't worry, Mrs. Patman, I can assure you that you won't find a trace of shells in lobster *al* Denise."

Denise shot him a warning look.

"Well, we'll clear out of here and let the two of you get back to work," Mr. Patman said. "I'm sure you must have plenty to do."

"Yes." Mrs. Patman slipped her pale hand into

the crook of her husband's strong, tanned arm. "But don't work too hard. Make yourselves at home. It's OK to have a little *fun*."

Denise felt her face grow hot once again. Mrs. Patman *had* seen them after all!

When the Patmans left, Denise sank into the nearest chair. She didn't feel like playing games anymore. *I'm no rich society woman dabbling in the kitchen on the maid's night off*, she told herself. *I'm a broke college student—worse than broke. I'm a very much in debt college student. And I'm here to work. So I'd better get to it.*

But as she began to fill dishes of radish roses and carrot curls with ice water, tears swam in her eyes. *What if the Patmans aren't fooled by the fake lobster? What if they make a scene? Even worse*, she thought, blinded by visions of some medieval debtor's prison, *what if they refuse to pay me?*

Chapter Four

"Yuck, it's still raining," Elizabeth complained as she and Scott left the journalism building that housed the *Gazette* offices.

"Then stay here with me," Scott suggested. He caught her by the hand and pulled her back inside.

She shook her head and laughed. Although she hadn't done a thing she meant to do at the *Gazette*, the time she'd spent with Scott had cheered her considerably. She was feeling much more optimistic and lighthearted. "It's tempting, but I've got a date with Professor Young." She kissed Scott on the end of his nose. "And I've got to hurry. I'm going to be late as it is."

"So what? Who'd know? It's a huge seminar in a dark auditorium. How many people are going to show on a Saturday afternoon when it's pouring rain?"

"All the more reason for me to go."

Scott rolled his eyes. "And what are those points

going to earn you? Honestly, Liz, who's going to notice you're there?"

"Oh, I don't know," she said, popping open her umbrella. "Why would anyone notice a soaking wet girl stumbling through a dark auditorium, climbing over seats and whacking people with a gargantuan backpack and a dripping umbrella?"

"Well, maybe you have a point, but I still wish you'd stay here with me." Pushing her umbrella to one side, he pulled her back into his arms.

She giggled and surrendered to his kisses for a few moments. Then she pulled away again. "Go to lunch!" she teased.

Scott let his lower lip droop comically before obediently ducking out into the rain.

Laughing, she waved good-bye. Then she dashed away in the opposite direction.

"Elizabeth!" she heard someone shout.

Did Scott forget something? Because her umbrella blocked most of her view, she had to spin her whole body around to look for the source of the voice. Through the driving rain she saw Tom Watts charging down the sidewalk toward her.

What is going on? she wondered. *Everywhere I turn today, there he is. And he looks* awful! She shuddered. His scruffy appearance went far beyond someone who'd gotten caught in the rain. He was filthy and unshaven—wild looking, like some deranged vagrant. She tilted her umbrella to block his gaze and speeded her pace.

"E-liz-a-beth!" he bellowed.

He sounded so pathetic, she couldn't help but pause and look back again. *What has happened to him?* she thought with disgust. *Never in my wildest nightmares could I have imagined Tom like this.* Not only was he freakish looking, with mud on his face and his hair dripping into his eyes, but he was acting crazy as well—like someone strung out on something. *This is probably Dana Upshaw's influence. As wacky as she is, she probably got him hooked on drugs.*

As Tom limped steadily toward her Elizabeth realized that he'd already closed up much of the distance between them. With a gasp she spun around and scurried away. He was beginning to scare her.

"Elizabeth, wait! I have to talk to you!" He leaped from the sidewalk and cut across the muddy lawn.

From the corner of her eye she saw him splashing, slipping, and sliding closer and closer. Horrified, she turned her fast walk into a jog and then into an out-and-out run. *How dare he embarrass me like this?* she thought, revolted.

The light was already yellow as she reached the campus's busiest intersection. A quick look behind her told her that Tom was still there, still gaining on her. With her heart thudding in her chest as if the very devil were after her, she barreled through the crosswalk just as the traffic began to move. She made it, but Tom was caught. From the other side of the busy four-lane street she could see him stomping like an angry Rumpelstiltskin dancing around his fire. Still, Elizabeth wasn't taking any chances. She kept on running. She only hoped the traffic would be heavy enough to keep him on that side of the street long enough for her to escape.

Not daring to look back again, Elizabeth turned the corner and dashed across the stone piazza that skirted the art building. She was in such a hurry to get inside, her umbrella caught on the edge of the door and nearly turned wrong-side out. She struggled to shut it but couldn't. Fear, embarrassment, anger—it all was too much, but her frustration topped it off. With an aggravated grunt she yanked the bent umbrella free and stuffed it into the nearest trash can before sprinting down the hall.

Why does Tom keep hassling me? she wondered furiously. *For weeks he's taken every possible opportunity to humiliate me, hurt me, and degrade me. I can't take much more of this.*

Just outside the lecture auditorium she ducked into a niche that held a pay phone. *The sooner I can get away from SVU, the sooner I'll be free of Tom's harassment,* she reasoned. She fumbled her backpack off her shoulders and dug into the side pocket for change. Scott wouldn't have had time to make it back to his dorm, but she decided to leave a message on his machine.

She winced at the painfully loud beep. "Scott—" She licked her lips, which somehow seemed to be the only dry spot on her whole body. "Scott, I've changed my mind. I really would like to leave for Denver . . . as soon as possible. . . ." Hearing a noise at the end of the corridor, she added hurriedly, "Now! I want to leave *immediately.*" She slammed down the receiver, peeked timidly into the hallway, and sighed with relief. It was just another student hurrying in from the rain. Maybe she had lost Tom after all.

As she reached for the auditorium door handle her breath seemed to whoosh out of her body, leaving her dizzy and weak. *What have I done?* she thought. *Am I going crazy? I can't leave tomorrow. I have to call him back!*

The lights went off on the other side of the door, indicating the seminar had begun. She glanced at the clock on the wall. *Oh, well, I don't have time to do anything about it right now,* she told herself. *I can call him back later and explain what happened. Scott probably won't get his messages before I get out of class anyway. Besides, he couldn't possibly take me seriously. I must have sounded like a real crackpot.*

But even if he does, what of it? she thought as she tiptoed into the dark auditorium. There was nothing keeping her at SVU. Tom and Jessica, the two people she loved most, had devastated her. Besides, there was nothing wrong with showing the world she meant business.

Why did I think this was such a good idea? Jessica asked herself as she stumbled along the sidewalk, trying to balance a huge bouquet of flowers in her arms and hold an umbrella at the same time.

As soon as Elizabeth had left the room Jessica

71

had headed for the nearest flower shop. Despite Elizabeth's words that she was forgiven, Jessica knew that she still had a long way to go to get back in her sister's good graces. She'd told the guy at Buds and Blossoms that she wanted a big bouquet, but she was beginning to think that maybe he'd overdone it just a tad.

But Elizabeth would *have* to forgive her when she saw this colorful collection. The flower guy had thrown in a little of everything: daisies, lilies, rosebuds, carnations, peonies, and even a bunch of flowers Jessica had never heard of. The muscles in her arm were practically screaming from strain.

There's no way I'm lugging this thing all the way to the dorm, she thought as she turned left and headed across the quad. *The* Gazette *offices are lots closer. But she'd better appreciate the fact that I trudged all this way in the rain to give them to her.*

Jessica had just passed the library when the rain stopped. *At least I can get rid of this stupid umbrella now,* she noted. *If I . . . can . . . get it . . . down.* As she wrestled to close the umbrella with one hand she nearly dropped the flowers. Suddenly she let out a gasp of surprise as someone took the umbrella from her and closed it.

"Eew! What happened to you?" she asked when she found herself looking up into the filthy face of none other than Tom Watts. He looked as if he'd just lost his last round in a mud-wrestling tournament.

"Have you seen Elizabeth?" he asked hastily.

"Just because you're mad at me about last night doesn't mean you have to shout at me," Jessica complained.

"Jessica, I don't know what that was all about last night—I'm not even sure I *want* to know—but I'm not in the mood for games. I have to talk to Elizabeth *now!*" Tom gave her a bloodshot glare. He looked positively crazy. "Where is she?"

"I don't have her whole schedule memorized, Tom." But judging from the look on his face, she didn't want to bait him more than necessary. "I think maybe she's at the *Gazette* office—it's where she usually is these days. That's where I'm headed, if you must know. I'm taking her these flowers."

"No, she's not at the *Gazette*. I just saw her leaving there."

"If you *saw* her, then why didn't you *talk* to her?"

"I tried, but I . . . well, she ran, and I lost her in the rain. I thought maybe you'd know where she'd be."

"I told you. I don't know!"

"Jessica, this is important. I have to talk to her before she leaves."

"Leaves what?"

Tom growled and waved her own umbrella at her. "Leaves *here*. SVU. Isn't she still planning to go to Denver?"

"That's not till the end of the semester, Tom. You know that." Jessica couldn't keep the annoyance out of her voice. Why was everyone always reminding her that her sister was leaving? "But go home and change clothes first, OK? You're *sooo* disgusting. I don't blame Elizabeth for running away from you."

"Wait—did you say you were taking those flowers to Elizabeth?"

"I said I was taking them to the *Gazette*. You're the one who said she wasn't there, brainiac."

"Who are they from? Scott?" Tom seemed to turn a jealous green before her very eyes.

"If you *must* know, they're from me. They're a peace offering to get her to forgive me for the kissing thing last night."

Tom closed his eyes and shook his head. "No telling what she thinks that was all about."

"I explained it to her this morning."

Tom's eyes blinked back open. "That should have been interesting. I wouldn't have minded sitting in on that little explanation myself. Why on earth did you do it, Jess?"

"Here, hold these a minute," she said, shoving the flowers at him. She dug in her shoulder bag for a Kleenex. "Wipe your face. I can't have a serious conversation with you standing there looking like the abominable mud man."

He handed the flowers back to her and wiped his face. His efforts only made him look worse.

"OK, about last night. It's really very simple—"

"Whoa, whoa. Help me out here, Jess. I must have mud in my ears because I don't see how this fiasco could be *simple*."

"Well . . . I just thought . . . well, I know you

still love Elizabeth. . . ." Jessica squirmed under Tom's glare. "And she still loves you."

Tom rolled his eyes.

"She *does*, Tom. A sister knows these things. Well, anyway . . . I know you want to get back together, but both of you are too stubborn to make the first move. I thought if I pretended to be Elizabeth, I could give you both a little jump start in the right direction. But then when you kept kissing me, I just panicked."

"Sorry it was so awful for you."

Jessica blushed. "It *surprised* me. I didn't say it was awful. Actually it was just the opposite. Don't let this go to your head, Tom, but you're a darn good kisser. I know a lot of guys who could take lessons and still not be in your league."

The look of amazement on Tom's face caused her to stifle an embarrassed giggle. She could hardly believe it herself. Here she was admitting right to Mr. Yawnworthy's face that he was a good kisser. She glanced around sheepishly. "Anyway, your kisses . . . threw me a little. When I realized how powerful your feelings were for Elizabeth, I knew I couldn't play games."

Tom looked at her with newfound hope in his eyes. He almost began to look a little cleaner. "You aren't kidding me, are you, Jess? Because I'm way beyond humoring you. I know you've never thought much of me—"

"Don't be silly, Tom. I've always thought you

were the perfect guy for Elizabeth. Seriously. I was honestly trying to get the two of you back together last night." She softened her tone. "I'd do anything to help."

"Anything?" he asked.

She nodded. She'd already kissed the guy. Didn't that prove something?

"Then let me take those flowers to her."

Jessica hugged the flowers to her chest possessively. "Mmmm . . . I don't know."

"C'mon, Jess, after your little masquerade you owe me."

She hung her head guiltily. "I guess I do."

Tom handed Jessica back her umbrella in exchange for the bouquet. "Thanks, Jessica. I hope these flowers will change her mind enough that . . . that she'll at least *listen* to me."

I hope they'll change her mind about more than that, Jessica thought. *You're my last hope, Tom. If you can't convince Elizabeth to stay, no one can. Not even me.*

Cradling Jessica's flowers, Tom did an about-face and headed back to the *Gazette* offices. As he walked he breathed in the bouquet's tangy, sweet fragrance. The blooms were so fresh and delicate, yet they were sturdy. Like Elizabeth herself. Surely she wouldn't run from him again after he brought her a peace offering as beautiful as this.

Tom groaned, hardly believing his eyes. There, splashing across the quad in his direction, was

Dana Upshaw *again!* She was clearly searching for someone, and Tom knew instinctively he was the intended victim.

Hide! he told himself. His eyes darted around, anxiously seeking cover. He felt utterly exposed and defenseless. *I can't let her see me. I know the way her mind works. If she catches me now, she'll assume the flowers are for her. And as guilty as I feel for the way I treated her this morning, I'll hand them over like a big dope.*

He considered hightailing it back to his dorm, but he had almost reached his destination. He couldn't stop now—not when he was so close. Holding the bouquet in front of his face like camouflage, Tom hurried the last few yards and dashed up the steps.

"Can I help you?" someone asked when he stepped through the door to the *Gazette* offices.

"Flowers for Elizabeth Wakefield," he mumbled from behind the bouquet.

The girl pointed to a desk and disappeared through another door.

Tom set the vase on the desk and carefully straightened the few flowers that had gotten slightly squashed in transit. It was then that he noticed the small white envelope dangling from one of the flowers. In Jessica's wide, swirly handwriting it read, Elizabeth.

Whoa! Good thing I noticed that in time, he thought. *It wouldn't have done me much good to lug these flowers all the way over here if Jessica still got all the credit.*

He yanked the white card from its snug little

envelope and stuffed it into his pocket. "Now, a note from me," he mumbled, opening the top desk drawer in search of a slip of paper. The drawer was practically empty, but he found a stub of a pencil. In the second drawer he found a note card, tore it in half, and wrote: *I'm sorry. Please let me explain. I love you*. And signed it, *Forever, Tom*.

He slipped his own note into the envelope and sat there glumly until the door opened and more *Gazette* staffers began to filter in. With one last look of hope at the flowers he slipped out of Elizabeth's chair and ducked out of the newspaper office unseen.

Elizabeth slumped in her seat in the back row of the lecture hall. Far below her in the darkened auditorium a slide flashed on the pull-down screen.

"And here we have Monet's *Sunrise*," droned Professor Young, who was anything but what his name implied. His students joked that he must have been around when the paint on Monet's canvases was still wet.

Elizabeth blinked and tried to focus on the projected painting. She knew the blurriness reflected back at her wasn't entirely because *Sunrise* was a work of impressionism. The way her eyes kept filling with uncalled-for tears, her whole world had become an impressionistic blur.

When she sniffed rather loudly, Ahmed, a Pakistani

student who sometimes borrowed her notes when he had trouble understanding the professor, turned and looked up at her.

"I got caught in the rain," she whispered, wiping the tears and raindrops away with the back of her hand.

He smiled politely and turned his attention back toward the screen, where Mary Cassatt's painting *The Boating Party* was now being shown. As Professor Young narrated, Elizabeth jotted down into her notebook the name of the painting, the date it was completed, and the name of the artist. She could always look up the rest of the information in the text later.

The projector's light flickered, and a different work appeared on the screen. "And here we have *The Scream,* painted in 1893 by Edvard Munch," Professor Young intoned. "Note the stark horror. See how the subject in the foreground presses his hands to his head as if to keep his very skull from bursting with anguish."

Elizabeth stared at the misshapen human form on the screen. Was it a man or a woman? She couldn't tell, but she could relate to how it felt. The bulbous-headed person was running away from something terrifying, just as she herself had. Its pasty face seemed to show not merely fear but mental torment. She saw a creature who was reaching the breaking point—a person who felt exactly the way she'd felt over the last few days.

"Note how the subject's inner conflict is intensified

by the swirls of red, green, and yellow in the background. . . ."

Elizabeth wanted to let loose the same agonized scream. All because of Tom Watts.

Munch's painting disappeared and another took its place. And then another and another. Slide after slide flashed onto the screen, accompanied by Professor Young's expressionless commentary, but Elizabeth's pencil lay still. She was no longer paying the least bit of attention. Just the thought of Tom's name had sent her into her own little world.

A huge lump lodged in her throat. *Jessica insisted that Tom thought he was kissing me,* she reminded herself. *But how could that be true? Doesn't he remember my kisses well enough to distinguish them from Jessica's?*

She remembered *his* kisses. It was a good thing she was sitting because the very thought of Tom's lips against hers made her weak in the knees. Her pulse sped up as she closed her eyes and recalled the thrill of being in Tom's arms. No one else had ever made her feel the way Tom did. No one.

Get a grip! she told herself angrily. *Forget about Tom. Scott is the man in your life now. He's the one you should be daydreaming about. He's the only one who really cares about you.*

The harder she tried to shove Tom from her mind, the more he filled her thoughts completely. The only time thoughts of Scott managed to squeeze in was when she found herself mentally comparing Scott's kisses to Tom's. Scott's some-how always came up lacking.

Elizabeth jumped as Ahmed pecked her lightly on the knee to get her attention. He pointed to the door. Following the line of his finger, she saw Scott's face pressed against the narrow, reinforced glass panel. He appeared to be motioning for her to come out into the hall.

What could he want? she wondered, annoyed to have been pulled from her thoughts. She climbed past the other students in her row and slipped from the auditorium as quietly as possible.

Scott was positively beaming. "I got your message," he said as the door shut behind her.

"What? Already?" she asked, astonished.

"Yes, already. On my way to the dining hall I stopped by my room for a dry shirt. When I heard you on the machine, I blew off lunch and got busy arranging our trip."

Suddenly her stomach clenched as if she'd just dropped from a roller coaster's highest peak. "Our trip?"

"Yes." If he noticed her surprise, he didn't show it. "It's all set. We're leaving tomorrow."

"Tomorrow?" she gasped.

"Will you quit acting like a parrot?" he teased. He grasped both her shoulders. "You've made me so happy, Elizabeth! I knew you'd come to your senses eventually and make the right decision. It was easy to see that despite all your protests, you were

81

really dying to leave. And now we are!" He pulled her tightly against his chest. "Isn't this exciting?"

Panic skittered up her spine like a chill. "But . . . but how can everything be all set? It hasn't even been an hour since I called." Her hands began to shake. "You couldn't have gotten reservations."

"Not reservations, *tickets*. Already bought and paid for. All I have to do is pick them up this afternoon from the travel agent's office. And then tomorrow we're off to Denver."

Elizabeth's jaw dropped in disbelief. He was certainly a fast worker. *How could this be happening?* she asked herself. *One phone call and suddenly I'm leaving tomorrow.* She couldn't take it in. "H-How c-could you have gotten tickets already?" she stammered feebly.

"It's like I've told you before. Anything is possible if you know the right people."

"Scott, I can't—"

"Don't do this again, Liz." He pressed his lips together into a tight line. "You can't keep changing your mind. It's time to move ahead, and you know it. After all, it was *your* idea."

I suppose he's right, she thought. *And I can't very well blame Scott, not when I was the one who made that insane demand in the first place.* "I—I know, but—"

He smacked his forehead. "Oh, I meant to tell you. I saw Tom Watts on my way over here, and you'll never guess who he was with—your sister!"

Hot tears rushed to her eyes, and she blinked them back angrily. With everything that was already going on in her mind right now, that should have been the last thing she wanted to hear. But it strengthened her resolve to leave even more.

"Sorry. I didn't mean to interrupt," Scott said casually. "Now, what were you saying?"

Elizabeth took a deep breath and struggled to calm herself down. "I . . . I was just going to say . . . well . . . I can't let you buy my ticket. You've done so much already."

"No problem. Consider it my going-away present."

"But—"

He touched his finger to her lips. "Not another word. I'm happy to do it."

She pulled his hand away. "But you shouldn't have to do everything. I—"

He kissed the top of her head. "You're sweet. And you're right. I'm going to be really pressed for time this afternoon. Besides picking up our tickets, I wanted to call the shipping company and order packing boxes to be delivered to our dorms. And I have my own packing and all to do. I'll tell you what. You could really help me out by typing up my last *Gazette* piece."

Elizabeth frowned. She was reminded of all the times she'd been asked by friends—and especially her sister—to do their homework. It had always made her feel uncomfortable.

"Hey, don't give me that look. It's no big deal, just a little profile of that new leisure-studies professor. It's all written up in that file folder on our desk. If you could just type it up for me, it'd free me for more important matters—like our future!" He grabbed her up into another hug, this time practically squeezing the breath out of her, but she was too numb from shock to feel it.

"OK," she conceded. She had plenty of her own work to do, but she couldn't very well say no, considering all the things he was doing for her.

As Elizabeth slipped back into the auditorium she was surprised to find that her seminar was over. For a moment she stood there listening to the familiar sounds of squeaking chairs, rustling notebooks, and shuffling feet. It took her a while to snap out of it, but once she did, she gathered up her books and took off in search of Jessica. She had to tell her the news as soon as possible, before someone else told her. For better or worse, she was leaving tomorrow.

With a grinding of gears Denise whipped Winston's orange Volkswagen into the Mighty Mart parking lot. *Thank goodness Winston didn't hear that!* Denise thought as the engine coughed to a halt. *The way he babies this old junker, he'd probably never let me drive it again.*

"Well, too bad," she grumbled. "I wouldn't be driving it now if he hadn't forgotten that stupid poppy seed dressing. I have a million and one things to do at the Patmans', and where am I? Shopping at Mighty Mart!" She slammed the car door. "I love you to death, Winnie, but sometimes, like *right now,* I could just strangle your skinny neck."

As she splashed across the puddle-dotted parking lot she was glad the rain had finally stopped. The humidity was causing her naturally curly hair to frizz. She unconsciously reached up and smoothed down the waves she'd tried so hard to tame. At the rate she was going, she was going to be so frazzled by the time she got this dinner done that she'd scare the guests to death serving it. But it'd all be worth it once she got paid.

She skidded to a halt and waited for the automatic door to open. Those silly things were always slower than she was. She couldn't count the times she'd nearly crashed right into them.

When the door finally slid open, Denise could hardly believe her eyes. The Mighty Mart was stiflingly crowded, even for a Saturday afternoon. *What is it? A two-for-one sale on pork 'n' beans?* she wondered as she elbowed her way through the crowd and ducked around the side of the checkout counter.

Suddenly a flashbulb went off somewhere close enough to cause blue spots to swim before her eyes. When she could focus again, she saw a burly man backing toward her, a video camera held high on his shoulder. Denise ducked behind a floor display of paper products as he and a huddle of noisy people surged past. Everyone seemed to be shoving microphones into the face of a pudgy, red-faced man who was wearing the starched white shirt, black tie, and red vest that indicated he was a Mighty Mart employee. Embroidered in fancy script on the vest was the word *Manager*.

"Isn't this exciting?" tittered a woman with two little kids in her shopping cart.

"What's going on?" Denise asked.

"Mickey, don't open the Crunchy O's yet. Sit down before you fall." The woman turned from her son back to Denise and whispered, "It's *Hal Horner*. Right here in our very own neighborhood."

"Hal Horner, the investigative reporter?"

"Yes. Don't you think he's more handsome in person than on TV? I think he is just the cutest thing! My husband is probably wondering what's happened to me, but I absolutely refuse to leave without seeing what's going on. I've been walking up and down these two aisles for the past fifteen minutes. . . . Angela, let go of your brother's hair!"

Denise craned her neck to see around a pyramid of paper towels as two uniformed policemen ushered the manager through the front door. The media circus that always surrounded one of Hal Horner's consumer rip-off revelations poured out into the parking area.

Denise almost tumbled headfirst over the display when a woman with a pouf of snow white hair bumped against her with her cart.

"Did you see that?" she shouted to the woman with the kids, waving one arm dramatically despite the bulky tapestry purse dangling from it. "They're carting Ralph away. Serves him right, I'd say."

Denise turned her attention back to Hal Horner as he positioned himself so that his camera crew could shoot him with the manager being led toward the police car in the background.

Hal was shorter and thinner than she'd imagined after seeing him on TV, and his prematurely gray hair was startling in person. But as the woman said, he *was* more handsome in real life than on TV in an older-man, distinguished kind of way, even though his dark bronze tan looked fake.

He nodded for the cameras to roll. "And another swindler out to defraud the unsuspecting consumer has been brought to justice. Remember," he proclaimed, lifting his index finger in a gesture that always proceeded his famous tag line. "If you've been hornswoggled, call Hal Horner! I'm the man on your side."

Denise focused again on the scene in the parking lot. A policeman reached out to protect the manager's balding head from hitting the door as he was tucked into the backseat of the police cruiser.

"What did the poor guy do?" Denise asked the two women.

"This store has been selling scrod as flounder," the older woman explained, turning up her nose in disgust.

"What nerve!" the mother gasped incredulously. "Angela, please sit still."

"Imagine us having to pay the price of flounder and getting cheap codfish!"

As the two women delved into a heated discussion about the unfairness of big chain stores cheating hardworking, honest shoppers, Denise moved away toward the condiment aisle. *Scrod? Flounder? What's the difference?* she thought. *Fish is fish, isn't it?*

After a beat she felt the familiar tug of her conscience. *But fish isn't tofu, and neither is lobster.* She groaned. *Oh, if I can just get through this dinner party, I'll never do anything this stupid again. I swear!*

She snatched a generic bottle of poppy seed salad dressing off the shelf but then reconsidered. The Patmans would notice things like that. She replaced it and picked up Wimberly & Windsor's, the most expensive name brand. "Better not push my luck," she mumbled.

When she got to the checkout counter, Hal was still standing nearby, talking with his camera crew. For a brief moment he looked her way, and his steely gray eyes seemed to bore right into her. *Uh-oh*, she thought. *He knows about the tofu. He's going to turn his camera on me and—*

Quickly Denise shoved money into the checker's hand, snatched the dressing bottle from her, and hurried out. If Hal Horner and those two women could get this worked up over fish labels, Denise could hardly imagine what they'd do if she served them paprika-covered tofu instead of rock lobster tails. Embarrassing her on the five o'clock news would only be a start. She imagined that Hal wouldn't be satisfied until he'd branded her with a huge *H* right in the center of her forehead. *H* for hornswoggler!

But by the time she got the VW in gear, she'd

pushed her concerns aside. After all, she wasn't catering a dinner for Hal Horner. She was serving lobster *al* Denise to the Patmans. And if Bruce, who was always bragging about his discriminating rich tastes, couldn't tell the difference, then neither would his parents. Right?

Chapter Five

"Elizabeth!"

Elizabeth tensed up and froze in the middle of the quad. *Oh, not Tom again!* she thought. She nervously glanced over her shoulder but was relieved to see Todd Wilkins jogging to meet her.

"Hey," he said casually. "Where are you off to in such a hurry? You look like you're trying out for the SVU track team."

"I probably could. It seems all I do anymore is run in circles. I just finished making a circuit from Dickenson Hall to Theta house, then to the student union and around to Isabella's, and now I'm on my way to the Red Lion."

"Tracking down Jessica?" Todd laughed.

She grinned. "How'd you ever guess?"

"I noticed you didn't mention many buildings where there might actually be classes going on." He pushed his baseball cap farther back from his face. "Have you tried the Sweet Valley Mall?"

"I probably should have looked there first." Elizabeth suddenly felt better than she had all day. It was great seeing Todd again.

"Are you in a big hurry?"

"Uh . . . no, not really." She glanced at her watch. "But I need to find Jessica before . . ." She wanted to tell Jessica about her updated travel plans before someone else did, but she didn't want to send Todd away. It seemed as if it'd been ages since they'd talked one-to-one.

Todd held out his arm. "Come on, what do you say? Let's take a walk. Let Jessica come find *you* for a change."

"OK." Elizabeth slipped her hand in the crook of Todd's arm. "Lead the way."

It felt like old times as she and Todd crossed the quad and headed down the sidewalk that led to the athletic fields, one of Todd's favorite places.

"Are you tired?" he asked. "You want to sit awhile?"

Elizabeth nodded.

Todd led her to a concrete bench outside the practice gym. It was still wet from the rain, so they walked over to the soccer field and sat on a section of bleachers that had been protected from the rain by the press box.

"I've got that shoulder you were asking about right here." Todd smacked one of his broad, strong shoulders.

"You got my message, huh?" Elizabeth said sheepishly. "I guess I was feeling down and—"

"You don't have to make excuses, Liz. Anytime you need to talk, I'm here for you. You know that. So go ahead and tell old Todd what's bugging you."

That invitation and a single encouraging look were enough to make her spill out all her doubts and worries about leaving SVU.

"I keep telling myself this is a once in a lifetime opportunity," she concluded. "DCIR is supposed to be *the* place to learn investigative reporting techniques, but I'm not so sure I'll be able to handle it. I mean, I know I can handle the work, but I don't know about leaving Jessica and all my friends behind."

"Liz, if you feel it's the right thing to do, then I'm sure it is. You are one of the most levelheaded people I've ever known." He brushed a strand of hair away from her face. "It was one of the things I always loved about you."

It felt strange that she could hear words like *love* coming from Todd's mouth and not have her heart skip a beat, but it seemed they'd finally reached that point where they really were just destined to be good friends.

"You know, we're all going to be sad at the end of the semester when you leave—"

"Actually . . . that's the next thing I was going to tell you. There's been a change of plans. I . . . I guess I'm leaving tomorrow."

Todd let out a low whistle. "Tomorrow? That's sort of short notice, isn't it?"

"I know. I can hardly believe it myself."

He shook his head. "That doesn't sound like you,

Liz. You aren't the type to just pick up and move."

Elizabeth smiled wistfully. No other guy understood her the way Todd did.

"I know, but I've decided it's best to go ahead and leave now. I'm only making Jessica crazy, and Tom—"

"Tom? Have you talked to Tom Watts?"

"No, but Jessica has this crazy idea that if she can get us back together, I won't leave."

"Any chance of that happening?"

Elizabeth shook her head sadly. "I'm dating Scott Sinclair now," she added, not wanting to sound too pathetic.

"That's what I heard." Todd's face was unreadable, but for some reason Elizabeth gathered that Todd wasn't too impressed.

"How about you? Are you . . . well, dating anyone?" Elizabeth bit her lip nervously. Todd had been so crushed by Gin-Yung's death that she wondered if he'd ever be able to lead a normal life again.

Todd exhaled so hard, he seemed to shrink a few inches. "No one right now. I don't think I'm ready for a full-time girlfriend. I still think about Gin-Yung. It's hard to let go. Even when you know someone's gone forever."

"I know," Elizabeth said, falling into his arms for a long, comforting hug, hoping it wouldn't be their last.

Jessica sat at a table in the Red Lion Café, idly stirring a cup of mocha java while her best friend, Lila

Fowler, chattered on and on about some dinner party.

"Uh-huh," Jessica uttered without the slightest idea what Lila had just asked.

Lila tossed back her long dark hair and rolled her eyes dramatically. "Are you going to stir that all day or drink it?"

"Huh?" Jessica blinked. "Oh, I'll drink it when it cools some."

"Jess, you've been clinking your spoon back and forth in that cup for ten minutes. It's not going to get any cooler unless you ice it down."

Jessica smiled weakly. "I guess I hadn't noticed."

"I guess not."

Jessica took a sip to satisfy her best friend, then turned her attention back to the door. Had Elizabeth gotten the flowers? Had Tom convinced her to stay? She couldn't keep her mind straight.

"Jessica Wakefield! Are you listening to me at all?"

"Huh? Oh yes. Sure, Lila. I'm listening."

"Prove it. Tell me one thing I've said to you in the last five minutes." Lila tapped her long scarlet fingernails on the tabletop.

Jessica began to fish for words like a fake psychic in a carnival. "Uh, you said you . . . and Bruce . . ." Seeing wrinkles form between Lila's perfectly shaped eyebrows, Jessica knew she was on the wrong track. "You . . . bought a new outfit . . . at . . . the Mystique. . . ." Again Lila's expression darkened. "I mean, at . . . Evita's Boutique."

"Hmmm. I guess you *were* listening," Lila admitted

with surprise. "Anyway . . . it's the most *scrumptious* outfit. The hostess pants are topped off by this narrow matching vest. The whole thing is olive sand-washed silk, and . . ."

Jessica tuned out her best friend again. She hadn't really been listening at all, but it was fairly easy to figure out what Lila had been talking about. Her entire conversation repertoire consisted of three subjects: Bruce Patman, clothing, and money.

Jessica fidgeted in her chair. She imagined her sister locked in a passionate embrace with Tom. Between his charm and *her* flowers, surely Elizabeth couldn't resist.

"So," Lila said, finishing off her raspberry fizz with a final little slurp. "What are you wearing tonight?"

"Tonight?"

"Jessica, where's your head? *Yes,* tonight. What are you wearing to the dinner party at the Patmans'?"

"What dinner party?"

"Are we having a communication problem here or *what*? The dinner party I just spent *ten minutes* telling you about. The one at the Patmans' house. The one Denise and Winston are catering?" Lila snapped her fingers in front of Jessica's face. "The one I just invited you to. Don't you remember that ecstatic 'uh-huh' you gave me?"

"Oh, *that* party. I don't know, Li. After last night I think I need to stay home with Elizabeth. We—"

"Elizabeth is going to be there."

Jessica dropped her spoon with a clatter. "What?"

"Well, I assume she is. Bruce mentioned that

he'd invited Scott Sinclair, and those two are joined at the hip these days."

"Oh yes, *now* I remember," Jessica said, not wanting to let Lila know her sister hadn't kept her posted on her plans. She nodded wisely and took a sip of her cold coffee.

"So? Are you and Nick coming to the party or not?"

"Yeah, sure. I guess," Jessica said distractedly.

"What are you going to wear?"

Jessica shrugged. Usually she would have spent quite a bit if time before any important function planning out her attire, but truthfully, she didn't even care if she went to this party. Not now. Not with Nick acting as if he was possessed by the spirit of lawyers past. And *especially* not if Elizabeth was going to be there with Scott. If she was there with Scott, that meant Tom hadn't gotten through to her.

I told him to go home and clean up first! she thought angrily. She remembered the way he'd looked at the party last night. Now *that* Tom, Elizabeth surely couldn't have said no to. Jessica's breath caught in her throat as she remembered the look in his dark brown eyes and the hoarseness in his voice as he proclaimed his love to her. She shivered, remembering the passion in his kiss.

The peck of Lila's nail on the table in front of her broke Jessica away from her memory. "OK, Jess. What's that old saying—a penny for your thoughts? Well, I'll up it to a quarter, allowing for inflation, if you'll tell me what's causing those deep concentration wrinkles across your forehead."

There was no way Jessica could tell Lila that she'd actually been thinking about Tom, not for a truck-load of pennies or quarters or even silver dollars. "I'm worried about Elizabeth," she admitted. "Things are going really wrong. She shouldn't be going to that party with Scott. Not when Tom—"

"Tom Watts? Jessica, you really *are* out of it today. Elizabeth and Tom broke up ages ago. They're hardly civil to each other anymore. Everybody on campus knows that."

"Tom and Elizabeth belong together."

"Nonsense. You always said Tom Watts was the most boring guy on the planet. Next to Todd Wilkins, that is."

Jessica shrugged. "So that makes them perfect for each other."

"Don't be silly. For once in her life Elizabeth has latched onto someone who can do her some good. Scott Sinclair has all kinds of connections. Did you know that his father is the chairman of the board of Morgan Media Holdings? He could really do won-ders for Elizabeth's career. She needs to forget about Tom Watts once and for all. Believe me, it's for the best."

"But Tom is—"

"Don't get me wrong. Tom's an OK guy, but he's basically a nobody. Elizabeth will be better off without him." Lila wiped her hands on a napkin with finality. "Speak of the devil . . . here she comes."

Jessica twisted in her chair to see her sister barreling toward them.

"Jess, I've been looking for you," Elizabeth said breathlessly. "I would have been here sooner, but I bumped into Todd as I was coming across the quad. You know how it is—we got to talking and time just slipped away. But anyway, wait till you hear my news." She pulled up a chair and plopped down at their table.

"You're not getting back with *him*, are you?" Lila asked.

Elizabeth squinted in Lila's direction. "What? Who, Todd? Of course not."

"Well, Jess said you and T—*ouch!*" Lila yelped as Jessica kicked her under the table.

"Lila, you know that Elizabeth and *Todd* are just good friends."

Elizabeth scooted closer and laid her hand on Jessica's arm. "Jessica, listen to me. I have something very important to tell you."

Jessica looked over at Lila and cleared her throat.

Lila bristled. "I hope you don't expect me to discreetly go to the ladies' room or something."

"What would be the point?" Elizabeth challenged. "We both know Jessica tells you everything anyway."

"True," Lila and Jessica admitted in unison.

"You might as well hear this now. It's about my going to Denver." Elizabeth clasped her hands and laid them on the table. "I've had a slight change of plans."

Jessica began to tremble with happy excitement.

Elizabeth was going to stay! "You saw Tom?" she asked giddily.

"Yes," Elizabeth acknowledged with a shake of her head. "But I don't want to talk about him. Listen—I'm not waiting until the end of the semester after all. I'm leaving for Denver tomorrow."

Tomorrow? All feeling drained from Jessica's body. She sat there speechless. It was all she could do to hold back her tears while Lila gushed and giggled over the news.

"It's *wonderful* to see you moving on with your life, Elizabeth," Lila exclaimed.

No, it's not, Jessica thought. *She's not moving on, she's moving away!*

Lila looked like a kid opening a birthday present. "This is perfect timing. We can celebrate tonight at the Patmans' dinner party," she announced grandly. "I'll make sure they break out their best champagne to toast your success. And Scott's too, of course."

Elizabeth reached across the table and took Jessica's hand. "I need you to be happy for me, Jess."

Jessica nodded, but she still didn't trust herself to speak. Her plan with Tom had failed. What could she possibly do in less than twenty-four hours?

Elizabeth hardly seemed to notice Jessica's uncharacteristic silence. "Come on back to the room when you and Lila are done here," she continued. "I really could use your help packing. I have so much

99

to do to get ready. I've got to run over to the *Gazette* first and finish a story, but I should be back in the room by three. I'll meet you there then, OK?"

Jessica nodded blankly.

After Elizabeth left, Lila hardly waited a beat before she dove into a story about Bruce Patman's new Porsche.

"Another black one," Jessica sneered. "How original. Like he hasn't had a black Porsche since the day he turned sixteen."

"Why are you so crabby?" Lila asked. "I know. You're jealous that Elizabeth is headed for new adventures while you're stuck here."

Why does everyone think they know me so well? Jessica fumed. "I'm not jealous. I'm just—"

"Well, you should be happy for your sister. Besides, without Elizabeth here to boss you around, you could be having some adventures of your own right here at SVU pretty soon." Lila grinned mischievously.

Frowning, Jessica reached across the table and tapped Lila's diamond-studded watch none too subtly. "Don't you have a hair appointment to get to?"

Lila rolled her eyes. "Fine. I can tell when you're trying to get rid of me, Jess. Go spend time with your sister, but try to wipe that gloomy look off your face. If not for Elizabeth's sake, then just remember that frowning causes wrinkles."

As soon as Lila was out of sight Jessica rushed to the pay phone. Her fingers shook as she flipped through the tattered campus directory, located the number she needed, and dialed it. She listened impatiently as a taped message informed her that Tom and Danny were out of the room.

"OK," she said with a sigh after the beep. "Tom, listen. This is important. There's been a big change in Elizabeth's plans. She's decided to leave for Denver *tomorrow!* You have to do something to stop her. Please, you *have* to!"

Dana paused in the doorway of the Red Lion Café and scanned the crowd. *Where is he?* she wondered. She laid one hand on the back of a nearby chair to steady herself as she caught her breath. Her other hand clamped down over the stitch in her side. She'd been running from building to building in search of Tom ever since she'd lost sight of him somewhere between Dickenson Hall and the journalism building.

When she stepped into the dim hallway, she saw a familiar blonde at the pay phone. *Thank goodness it's Jessica,* she noted. *She'll help me out.*

"Jessica," she shouted, rushing over. "Have you seen Tom?"

"No," Jessica said. "I was just trying to call him." Her eyes were red rimmed and watery. Obviously something had gone wrong.

"What's happened?"

"It's too awful."

"About Elizabeth—"

"Yes." Jessica nervously twirled a strand of hair around her finger.

"She saw Tom?"

"I think so, but . . . oh, *why* isn't Tom home? I have to tell him that Elizabeth is leaving tomorrow."

"*What*? Are you *crazy*?" Dana shrieked. "You can't tell him that! You're going to blow everything!"

Jessica's face darkened. "What are you talking about?"

"You know what I'm talking about—the *plan*. Boy, you can really act innocent when it serves your purpose, can't you?"

"I think you're as insane as Elizabeth says you are."

"And I think you're as unreliable as *everyone* says you are!"

"I can't believe this." Jessica grabbed a handful of napkins off a nearby table and began to blubber into them.

"Why are you so upset? Elizabeth is leaving. Isn't that what you *want*?"

"Of course not!" Jessica sobbed. "I love my sister—"

"Right." Dana put her hands on her hips. "We *all* do."

Jessica's eyes narrowed. "I do," she repeated in a steely, low tone. "And so does Tom . . . but I think you know that already."

Dana could only stare in angry bewilderment as Jessica brushed rudely past her and out the door.

That little witch! Dana thought, stomping her foot angrily. *That . . . that* traitor! *After playing*

102

undercover cop at Verona Springs, she thinks she has what it takes to be a double agent. She's been playing Scott for a chump all along.

Tom had once told Dana that Jessica wasn't as clueless as she liked people to think. Now Dana believed it. Scott had made a big mistake in trusting that conniving little flirt.

But not me. I'm not going to stab him in the back. I'll do whatever it takes to keep Elizabeth and Tom apart. Dana smiled. *After all, I'll only have to keep it up twenty-four more hours. Thanks, Jessica, for the important information.*

Scott must have written this in his sleep, Elizabeth thought as she deleted another paragraph from the story he'd asked her to type. It was awful. When he'd asked her to *type* it up, he should have said *write* it up. There was nothing in his file folder except a jumble of facts, figures, and quotes.

Well, she thought guiltily, *after all he's done for me lately, I guess I shouldn't complain.* Her fingers flew over the computer keys as she hurriedly shaped the information into an interesting article. When she paused to double check the spelling of Professor Odiwakki's name, she was distracted by the beautiful arrangement of flowers on her desk.

She sniffed deeply to take in their gorgeous perfume and smiled.

Karen Stokes, one of the new *Gazette* staffers, had pointed them out the minute Elizabeth walked in the door. "Some guy brought them!" she'd said excitedly. Elizabeth's heart had skipped a couple of beats as she wondered who they might be from. But evidently Karen had seen the delivery boy. An envelope with Jessica's loopy handwriting was hanging right there in plain sight.

Elizabeth ran a finger over one of the full pink peonies. It looked like a rose that had exploded. Jessica didn't have to go to all the trouble of sending her flowers, but still, it was awfully sweet. Too bad she wouldn't have more time to enjoy them.

Chapter Six

"Elizabeth?"

"Just a sec." Elizabeth finished typing in the last line of Scott's article and looked up to see Jeremy Bridges, a *Gazette* staffer, leaning against her desk. "What's up?"

"Well, ever since I heard you and Scott were going to DCIR, I've had a really important question I wanted to ask."

"Oh?" She couldn't imagine what serious, thought-provoking question Jeremy might have about DCIR.

"Can I have this desk when you and Scott are gone?"

She smiled up into his pie-shaped face. With his broad shoulders and thick neck, Jeremy looked more like a football player than a journalism major. She remembered how rude she thought he was when she'd first come to the *Gazette*, but she'd later come to realize he was a real sweetie inside.

"Sure—and sooner than you'd hoped. We're leaving tomorrow."

"Tomorrow?" His joking expression faded away. "Uh-oh."

"What's wrong?"

"Well, I *really* came over here to see if Scott finished that story on Dr. Odiwakki. Our illustrious editor is chomping at the bit for it."

"As a matter of fact, I've got it here on the computer now. I'll print it up and give it to Ed before I leave."

"Great, because I've gotta get back to the dorm. I was supposed to meet Shari twenty minutes ago. She's going to kill me. It's our anniversary, and I forgot."

As Jeremy turned to go, Elizabeth smiled at the image of big hulking Jeremy afraid of his tiny girlfriend. Shari Brown was only five feet tall and wouldn't weigh a hundred pounds on a fat day.

"Hey, Jer," she called him back. "I have an idea. Why don't you take this bouquet of flowers? Shari can't possibly be mad at you then."

"Naw, I couldn't take your flowers."

"My sister left them for me, but since I'm leaving tomorrow, I really won't have much time to enjoy them. Someone should get some use out of them. What do you say?"

"Well, Shari does love flowers. And pink is her favorite color."

"It's settled, then."

"Let me get something to put them in."

"No. Take the whole thing, vase and all."

106

"You're sure? Can I pay you for them?"

Elizabeth shook her head no and reached for the jangling phone on her desk.

"The *Gazette*," she answered. "Elizabeth speaking."

"Hey, Liz."

"Oh, hi, Scott. I was just finishing up here."

"I've got that flight information for you. Got a pencil handy?"

Elizabeth fumbled in the center drawer for a pencil while Scott started rattling off details. *No pencil!* Scott was always taking pens and pencils out of their desk and not putting them back. She shut the drawer and grabbed her book bag.

". . . Mile High Airlines. Flight three-fourteen," he finished just as she finally located a pencil. Elizabeth scribbled rapidly to catch up with the information he'd already given. Luckily her skills as a reporter enabled her to take notes quickly and remember details accurately.

"I'll get the taxi and pick you up at your dorm in the morning. You don't have to worry about a thing."

"Got it," she said, tucking her pencil behind one ear. "I still wish you'd let me help out with some of this."

Scott's reply faded into the background as she turned her attention to Jeremy, who was tapping on the desktop. He pantomimed picking up the flowers and pointed toward the door. Elizabeth nodded yes, but Scott diverted her attention by asking another question.

"What were you saying?" she said into the phone.

"I asked if you could be ready to leave for the

Patmans' party by six-thirty. That'll give us plenty of time to visit before dinner."

"OK, that sounds fine," she said, jotting down the time in her date book. Out of the corner of her eye she noticed that Jeremy was still patiently waiting. Holding the receiver against her ear with her shoulder, she scooted the flowers toward him. He scooped them up into his arms, whispered a thank-you, and took off.

As he headed out the door Elizabeth noticed the white envelope dangling from the bouquet. She tried to break into Scott's monologue to get him to hold on for a moment but couldn't. Suddenly Jeremy was gone before she had time to warn him.

I hope he takes Jessica's card off before he gives the flowers to his girlfriend, Elizabeth thought. Although she'd never gotten around to opening the envelope, she knew her sister. *No telling what kind of crazy apology Jessica wrote on that card.*

This is it! Nick thought as he snatched the large white envelope from the mailbox. He'd been anxiously awaiting the results of his college entrance exam scores since the moment he'd left the test site. But now that he actually held the scores in his hands, his heart began to pound and he felt slightly dizzy. He leaned against the brick planter full of purple and yellow pansies and fanned his face with the envelope.

If he hadn't been so darned nervous, he'd have laughed at the irony. After years of chasing criminals,

108

dodging bullets, and skulking down dark alleyways tailing suspects, Nick Fox was afraid of a little piece of paper.

Well, it was understandable. This little piece of paper could easily affect his whole future. Were his scores high or low? If they were low, then he couldn't get into college. If he couldn't get into college, then he couldn't go to law school. No law school, and he'd never be a lawyer. He'd have to go back to being a cop, and then what would happen to Jessica? He groaned at the thought.

He'd always liked being a cop. It was only after he'd started dating Jessica that he realized what a dangerous job he had—dangerous for her, that is. Thanks to some crazy notion of Jessica's that she should share every aspect of his life, she'd already had more close calls than he cared to think about. Her snooping into an undercover drug bust had landed her in jail. Her showing up at a chop shop bust had nearly gotten them killed. And her work at the country club . . . Nick shuddered. He didn't even want to think about how close he'd come to losing his beautiful Jessica.

"Never again, Jessica. I'd do anything to keep you safe," he vowed. "And here's the key to our future." He held the envelope up to the light, as if he could somehow read through the thick white cover without committing himself. He was torn between an urgent desire to see the scores and an extreme dread.

Overcoming the latter, he ripped into the envelope and pulled out the computer printout. His mathematics score jumped out at him. Math had never been his strongest subject, and it was the area he was most worried about. His score wasn't great, but it was well within the acceptable range required by the schools he'd been considering.

He scanned down the page. Reading—good. English—even better than he'd hoped for. Science reasoning—excellent! His heart started to pound. With these scores he wouldn't only be a shoo-in for acceptance at his dream schools; he could also possibly earn a scholarship or two.

Ecstatic, he dashed up the stairs to his apartment and dialed Jessica's number. She answered on the first ring. It was almost as if she'd been waiting for his call.

"Congratulations," she said after he'd told her the great news. But the tone of her voice wasn't coming across as very sincere. Nick felt some of his joy slip away like air from a leaky balloon. She of all people should be sharing his happiness. After all, he was doing this for her—for their future together.

"I have some college brochures I want you to go over with me later. I'd already narrowed it down to two choices, but actually I was shooting low. These scores are high enough to get me into almost any school I've looked at—even SVU. How would you like it if we were in some of the same classes?"

Nick was beginning to wonder if she was still on

the line. "Jess? Wouldn't that be romantic? We could study together and—"

"That sounds great, Nick."

"What's wrong? You don't sound very happy."

"Of course I'm happy. I knew you'd do fine."

"That's it? Just that you knew I'd do *fine?*"

"Sorry, Nick, but . . . I guess I have a lot on my mind."

Nick groaned. "What now?"

"You know."

"Are you going to let Elizabeth's leaving ruin the rest of the semester for you?" *Not to mention me,* he added mentally.

"I don't guess you have to worry about that anymore," Jessica said testily. "She's leaving tomorrow."

Nick was surprised to hear that. Elizabeth wasn't the type to do things on the spur of the moment, but if she'd made the decision, he knew she'd have a good reason. There was no sense in Jessica's worrying about it. "Well, you knew she was leaving," he reminded her. "Maybe this will make it easier for you, Jess, getting it over with sooner."

"*No,* it *won't!* I'm not ready for this, Nick. And to top it off, Lila wants me to go to some boring dinner party at the Patman mansion tonight."

"That sounds like an excellent idea. You need something to take your mind off your troubles. And besides, I'd be honored to escort you, my dear."

"Well . . . I was going to ask you, but I didn't think you would want to go. You told me you were sick to death of rich people after the whole Verona Springs deal, remember?"

"Oh, it wasn't really all that bad." Nick was hesitant to admit he was beginning to *like* hanging with Jessica's crowd. "Now that I have this test out of the way, I'm sort of looking forward to it," he added, peeking again at his test results. His chest swelled with pride. "I know this sounds weird, but since I've seen these scores, my self-confidence has gone up a notch or two."

"I didn't think you had any problems in the self-confidence department," Jessica said.

"I didn't as a cop. But I've been pretty nervous about whether I could handle college and law school. I think this party will be good for me, don't you? It'll give me a chance to see if I can hold my own with high-powered people like Bruce's dad."

"I don't know," Jessica whined. "I'm really not in the mood for partying."

"This is a switch," Nick joked. "Jessica Wakefield, not anxious to go to a dinner party! C'mon, Jess. Think about it. This is a prime opportunity to wow everyone with that new dress."

"What new dress?"

He laughed. "I know you, Jessica. You'll never convince me that you didn't run out to the mall and buy a new dress the minute you heard about this party."

"Maybe you don't know me as well as you think!"

He flinched at her snippy tone. "Well, I guess we *could* stay home tonight," he said rather guiltily.

"No," Jessica said weakly. "We have to go. Elizabeth and Scott will be at the party. It's the only way I'll get to spend any time with her at all."

"Jess, I know you're bummed about Elizabeth going away, but really it's for the best—"

"Well, if we're going to that dumb party, I have things to do," she interrupted. "I'll see you later." And she hung up.

As Nick replaced the receiver he felt sorry for Jessica. He knew how attached she was to her twin. *But sooner or later something like this had to happen,* he thought. *And I'm just glad I'm not the one coming between them.* He looked again at his scores and smiled. Things were going to be fine. As soon as Jessica realized she could get along without Elizabeth, the two of them would be free to plan their future together.

Hurry up and wait, Tom thought as he paced the sidewalk outside the journalism building, waiting for Elizabeth.

He ran his fingers through his clean, still wet hair. He'd just stepped out of the shower when he heard Jessica's message on the answering machine in his room in Reid Hall. She'd sounded so desperate, he'd toweled off, stepped into clean jeans and an SVU T-shirt, and run straight over.

Jessica must be mistaken, he thought. *Elizabeth can't leave tomorrow. Not without hearing what I have to say first.*

What was going on in Elizabeth's mind? It

didn't make sense. Elizabeth wasn't the type to just pick up and leave. Rash actions and snap decisions were more Jessica's style. Elizabeth was the type who always thought out her moves well in advance. This had to be Scott Sinclair's doing!

Unless it's yours, Tom, his conscience nagged at him.

"All the more reason for me to talk to her," he murmured.

At last she appeared. For a brief moment their eyes met—but she simply turned and walked away.

"Elizabeth!" he called, frustrated beyond reason. "Wait up!" But she didn't even pause. If anything, she sped up. "Please, Liz. Don't run away again. I've been waiting out here for an hour. Won't you at least hear me out?"

She paused but didn't turn; she just froze like a statue while he hurried to her side.

"Why do you keep following me?" she cried, whirling around to face him. Her face was blotched with angry red patches. "Why do you keep harassing me? Hounding me? *Stop* it, Tom!"

Tom shrank away from the anger in her tone.

Elizabeth held her clenched fists down at her sides. "I know you were angry at me. You've made that abundantly clear. If your goal was to hurt me, then you've succeeded. I'm hurt, OK? *Satisfied?*" Her aqua eyes glistened. She stepped back and took a deep breath.

"Elizabeth—"

"Can't you just leave me alone? Please, Tom.

For the sake of what we used to have, can't you show a little mercy and give me some peace?"

The tortured anger in Elizabeth's voice was too much for Tom to bear. He blinked rapidly to prevent a sudden gush of tears from his eyes. The speech he'd practiced a hundred times flew from his mind, leaving him paralyzed.

Say something, Watts, his mind screamed, but his throat wouldn't obey. *You can't let her leave SVU hating you. At least try to make her understand.* But Tom just stood there opening and closing his mouth like a fish out of water.

Elizabeth clenched her jaw. Her gaze practically dared him to speak, even to breathe.

"Elizabeth, p-please, j-just . . ."

Elizabeth faltered for a second. Then her cool blue-green eyes seemed to harden right in front of him. Without another word she spun on her heel and literally ran away from him, her ponytail bobbing with each step.

Getting that someone-is-watching-you prickle on the back of his neck, Tom turned. Dana was standing so close, his nose was tickled by her hair. *No wonder Elizabeth took off in such a hurry,* Tom thought in frustration. He quickly took a step backward to give himself room to focus.

"Hi!" Dana chirped. "You're certainly looking better. I hope that means your mood has improved since this morning. I was so worried about you."

A pang of guilt dug at his stomach. Dana was a

prize. How could she sound so cheerful after catching him with Elizabeth—again?

"You owe me a big apology," she cooed.

She was right, of course. "I'm sorry," he muttered.

She leaned against him. Pouting. Waiting.

"I—I was rude, but—" The words stuck in his mouth like old peanut butter. He *wasn't* sorry. He was mad. He hadn't asked Dana to follow him all over campus. It was her fault he'd missed Elizabeth this morning. And it was probably her fault Elizabeth had run away just now.

Dana ruffled her hands playfully through his wet hair until he suspected he looked like an electric shock victim. "I forgive you," she declared grandly.

Tom pulled away and tried to smooth his hair back into place. He felt weak with disappointment. He couldn't concentrate on Dana. All he could think about was how he'd let Elizabeth slip through his fingers again. He wanted to run after her, chase her to the end of the universe if he had to. Anything, if only he could just hold her one last time. "Dana, I've got to go," he mumbled, stepping away from her.

But he felt as if he'd hit a brick wall. Slowly he turned and found himself eyeball to eyeball with the smiling face of Bruce Patman.

"Hey, Tom!" Bruce clamped a hand on his shoulder, causing Tom's knees to buckle. "I've been looking for you, buddy. I'm always just missing you."

"He's pretty hard to keep up with," Dana teased. "I ought to know."

"I meant to ask you last night at Jessica's party, but, uh, well, you skipped out kind of early. Anyway, my folks are having a little dinner party tonight, and I was hoping you'd come."

"I don't think so, Bruce. I've been pretty busy at the station and . . ." Tom scratched his chin thoughtfully. He couldn't commit to making plans—not if Elizabeth was really leaving tomorrow. Tonight might be his last chance to talk to her.

"Aw, c'mon, man. You've got to. You know what a big football fan my dad is. We were just talking the other day about how much the team has changed, and he mentioned what a great quarterback you were back in your freshman year."

"That was a long time ago, Bruce. I don't play—"

"Oh, I know, but when I told my dad you were a friend, he *insisted* I invite you. He can hardly wait to show you off to his business associates."

Tom shook his head.

"C'mon," Bruce persisted. "*Consider* it at least. It won't just be a bunch of old guys. Winston and Denise are catering the affair, and Lila and I will be there, and where Lila goes, Jessica is sure to follow. Which means Nick. And of course there'll be a few guys you know from Sigma house. A whole bunch of the gang will be there—Elizabeth and Scott too."

Tom practically lost his balance as Dana stepped in closer and twined her arm tightly around his waist. "We couldn't possibly, Bruce," she declared.

117

"As Tom said, he's terribly busy, and I have a very important rehearsal I can't skip."

Tom's brain reeled. Elizabeth would be at the party, and Dana would be occupied elsewhere. This sounded too good to be true. Without Dana there to interrupt, he'd have all evening to get Elizabeth alone for a little talk. Elizabeth would never scream or run away in front of a roomful of civilized adults. Maybe he'd be able to have a real heart-to-heart talk with her at last.

"You know, now that I think about it," Tom said, tugging free of Dana's grasp, "I could use a night off. What time?"

"Drinks sevenish. Dinner at eight—"

"Eight o'clock?" Dana interrupted. "Well, why didn't you say so? That changes everything." She scooted between Tom and Bruce and tossed her dark hair over her shoulder. "I had no idea you'd planned to eat that late. Of *course* we'll be there."

"Great." Bruce looked at Dana strangely, but with typical Bruce Patman smoothness he covered his hesitation. "See you both there." He took a few steps away but turned back. "Strictly informal," he added.

When Bruce walked away, Tom whirled on Dana. But before he had time to ask her what her problem was, she smiled sweetly, leaned against him on tiptoe, and kissed him lightly on the lips. "See you at seven, OK?" She cocked her head flirtatiously as she stepped back.

He could feel the heat of his blood rising and knew his neck and ears were turning red. "I'm not driving out to your place to pick you up, Dana. In fact, I'm not—"

"I didn't ask you to, Mr. Grumpy. There's no sense in your driving all the way out to my house. I'll have to come back to campus and try to get in an earlier rehearsal anyway. Why don't I just meet you outside your dorm at seven? That'll give us plenty of time to get to the Patmans'."

He tried once again to tell her no, but Dana twisted every word he said into her own warped interpretation.

"Don't worry," she said. "The party won't really interfere with my practicing. If you want to go, then we'll go. You know I always try to please. I'll be waiting in front of your dorm right at seven. Don't be late."

As she skipped happily away Tom stood frozen in place, feeling as if he were about to have a nervous breakdown.

Chapter Seven

"Old lady outfit." Jessica held up one of Elizabeth's favorite suits. "Can't have too many of those in Denver." She wadded the suit into a ball and tossed it into a nearby packing box. Then she reached back into Elizabeth's closet. "Bo-ring. However, the fashion forecast says a Mister Rogers sweater is a *must* in the mountains this year. This baby goes to Colorado for sure." With a flick of her wrist Elizabeth's navy cardigan followed the suit into the box.

How long she'd been throwing Elizabeth's clothes haphazardly into boxes, Jessica didn't know. But she'd promised to help her sister pack, and so—like it or not—she was helping.

When she heard a key in the lock, she threw aside the brown jumper she was holding and turned anxiously toward the door.

Elizabeth hardly gave her a glance. With a

groan she dropped her backpack onto her bed and sank down beside it.

Jessica stood there about to burst with wanting to know about Tom.

"Uh . . . did you get the flowers?" she asked, skirting as close to the issue as she dared.

"Yes. They were very pretty. Thanks, Jess."

Jessica scratched her head in confusion. "Uh, but didn't To—"

"Oh, good," Elizabeth interrupted, seemingly aware of her surroundings at last. "The boxes are here." She jumped up from her bed and examined the nearest empty carton. "You know, Scott has been simply unbelievable through all this. I don't know what I would have done without him."

"Stayed here with your friends, probably," Jessica mumbled.

"He's gone to so much trouble for me," Elizabeth continued, obviously not catching a word Jessica said. "Making plans and reservations, buying the tickets, and now sending these boxes. He's even arranged to have everything picked up here at the dorm and shipped to Denver Monday afternoon. Isn't that great?"

"Yeah, great," Jessica muttered. "He's a real mastermind." *This is just too much!* she thought. *Tom gives Elizabeth a beautiful bouquet and all she can talk about is how classy Scott is for sending a bunch of cardboard boxes!*

Frustrated, Jessica began to rummage through

121

Elizabeth's closet again. She'd expected Elizabeth to come in all aglow, bursting with the news that she and Tom were back together.

Maybe Lila was right, she thought, heartbroken. *Maybe this* is *for the best. But it doesn't seem best. It doesn't even seem good. In fact, it seems positively tragic.*

Infuriated, Jessica scooped up a huge armload of shoes from Elizabeth's closet and angrily dumped them on top of the clothing she'd just packed.

"Jessica!" Elizabeth shrieked. "What are you doing? You can't pack that way!" She began yanking shoes from the box with both hands.

Jessica flashed teary eyes at her before stomping over to her side of the room.

Ashamed that she'd hurt her sister's feelings, Elizabeth softened her tone. "I'm sorry, Jess," she said. "I know you were just trying to help. I'm just . . . tired, I guess."

Elizabeth lined up three boxes. "Let's put clothes in this one." She marked the flap with a black marker. "Items to send back home in this one." She printed 72 Calico Lane neatly on the side. "And we can put shoes and purses and things that won't wrinkle in this one."

Elizabeth didn't dare look at Jessica. She didn't know how much longer she could keep this cheery expression pasted on her face. She was actually grateful she would soon be leaving. At least this tortured feeling of telling everyone good-bye would be over. More to keep busy than anything else, Elizabeth pulled the clothes out of the box Jessica had already packed and began to refold them. Everything was horribly wrinkled already.

Oh no, Elizabeth thought, *here's the suit Scott wanted me to wear to the party tonight! Well, maybe if I iron it, it'll be OK.* Jessica pulled a blouse from the box. "Here. Let me. I'll do it right this time. I promise."

Elizabeth couldn't say no. Jessica wasn't usually so helpful.

"OK. I'll start packing this other stuff." Elizabeth pulled out her top bureau drawer. There, stuck way in the back, tucked in among her pajamas, was another photo of her and Tom. *They're everywhere!* she thought. Her heart nearly broke as she flipped it over and read the words Tom had written on the back: *To my soul mate. I will always love you.*

Always *didn't last very long,* she thought bitterly.

In the next drawer she found a small wooden box full of costume jewelry. She found a shell bracelet that Tom had bought her at the beach. And a pair of earrings, little gold angels. He'd called her his angel before he'd started calling her a cheat and a backstabber.

She found the cartoon watch he'd given her. It'd been so funny. They'd gone to Pizza Paradiso to celebrate their one-month anniversary. They'd said no gifts. Tom didn't have much money then— it was before George Conroy had set up a huge trust fund for him. Then they'd both showed up with identical purple-wrapped boxes. Not only had they bought their gifts at the same shop; they'd bought each other the same gift. She wondered if Tom still had his. Probably not.

Then she pulled out the antique-cut steel locket he had given her. It wasn't expensive, but it was his very first gift to her. He'd given it to her after they'd worked together on a story that exposed dangerous secret societies on campus. It was supposed to commemorate her first big story, but it turned out to be a token of the day Tom had first told her he loved her.

The locket caught the light and glittered as it dangled from her hand on its silver chain. Elizabeth hesitated. "Here, Jess," she said quickly. "You want this stuff?"

"What stuff?"

"All this jewelry. I hardly ever wear any of it anyway." Elizabeth thought Jessica would be thrilled. She was always borrowing her things. But Jessica just stared angrily. "What's wrong?"

"I thought Tom gave you that."

Elizabeth shrugged guiltily. "Some of it . . . well, most of it, but I—"

"I can't believe you would just toss it out."

"I'm not tossing it out. I'm offering it to you."

"Same thing. I know what Tom meant to you. How can you stand there not caring about his gifts?"

Elizabeth threw the jewelry back into the drawer. "Give me one reason why I should."

"Because he loves you?"

Elizabeth leaned against the open drawer. "Tom

Watts doesn't love me. He never did." Her voice caught in her throat.

Jessica shoved a box out of her way with her foot. "Didn't you listen to a thing I said this morning? Tom told me—I mean, when he thought I was you, he said, 'Elizabeth, I love you.' Just like that."

"If he said it—which I *doubt*—then Tom was playing some kind of cruel joke on you. He doesn't love me, and I don't love him. Got it?"

"I can't listen to this anymore!" Jessica yelled. "I'm going to Lila's. You can just finish your own packing! I'm not going to help you ruin your life!" And she stomped out the door.

Elizabeth groaned. *Isn't this hard enough without Jessica acting like a brat?* she mused, snatching up the jewelry and looking for a place to put it. Her gaze traveled from a box to the wastebasket, finally falling on Jessica's bureau. Elizabeth crossed the room and emptied the whole jewelry box into the top drawer. *I could be gone a month before she ever notices it in that mess,* she thought.

However, just before shutting the drawer, she reconsidered and pulled Tom's locket out of the tangled mess. *Maybe I'll keep just this one piece,* she thought with a sigh.

Standing at the window and looking out at SVU's lovely campus, she held the cool, smooth locket against her lips and wished the next twenty-four hours to be over.

*　　*　　*

"I don't know. Maybe it's too stuffy looking." Tom leaned toward the small medicine-chest mirror and straightened his navy tie. The dark navy blazer and the khaki pants he was wearing had always been one of Elizabeth's favorite outfits, but he couldn't decide on a tie.

"How's this?" he asked, turning to face Danny.

Danny glanced up briefly from his political economy text. "Fine. Much better than the last four combinations you've modeled for me," he said with a teasing grin. "If you like the young accountant look."

Tom yanked the knot loose and pulled off the tie. "OK, laugh. Some friend you are." He tossed the blue tie onto his bed, which was so piled with discarded clothing it was beginning to look as if Jessica had been called in as the interior decorator. Tom continued to mutter, partly to Danny but mostly to himself. "I know I'm acting crazy, and my half of the room is beginning to look like a disaster area, but I can't help it. I've got to look just right tonight. This will probably be my last chance to talk to Elizabeth—maybe ever." Tom's heart nearly broke at the very thought.

He pulled out a tan tie with outlandish cartoon dogs all over it. "Yes! This is the one!" he said. "Elizabeth gave me this tie right after we finished the story on secret societies. Remember?"

Danny didn't answer, but as Tom slipped the tie around his neck, he remembered it as if it were yesterday.

"These are newshounds," Elizabeth had said, flashing him that famous Wakefield grin, complete with dimple. "This tie will always bring luck to the best TV newsman in the world." And then she'd kissed him.

He sighed slowly, deeply, remembering that kiss. *I hope you little pooches bring me luck tonight,* he thought, knotting the tie. "All right," he said, nodding at his reflection in the mirror. "I'm ready."

"Right," Danny said, laying down his textbook. "Cartoon tie—brilliant choice. I hear that's the ultimate in formal wear this season."

"Bruce said this dinner was informal."

Danny crossed his arms in mock seriousness. "Well, knowing Bruce, that could easily mean wearing your dress-down tux."

Frowning, Tom glanced toward his closet.

"Whoa, I'm kidding, Tombo. You look fine. You don't have time to change again anyway. It's nearly seven."

"What?" Tom yanked back his sleeve and looked at his watch, hoping Danny was wrong. "Six forty-five! Oh, great. I'm late. Dana will be here any minute."

Tom had planned to be long gone before Dana arrived, but he hadn't taken his necktie traumas into account. For once he had an understanding of why girls took so long to dress.

"Listen, if Dana comes up here looking for me, make some excuse, OK?"

"She's gonna be ma-ad!" Danny warned in a singsong voice.

"I know, but she'll just have to get over it. I can't have her there tonight. I have to talk to Elizabeth *alone*. I tried to level with Dana, but lately she hasn't been able to take no for an answer. Everywhere I turn, there she is, clinging to me like a flirtatious burr. I'm beginning to feel like a stalking victim."

"OK, I'll make excuses," Danny assured him, "You know me. Anything for true love."

Tom snatched up his keys and felt his pocket to make sure he had his wallet.

"Tell Liz that Izzy and I said hi. We'd be there too"—Danny held up his book—"but Charles Lindbloom has the lock on me this weekend."

"OK," Tom called back as he shut the door. Then to himself he added, "If she even gives me a chance to speak to her."

As he hurried across the parking lot he realized with a sinking stomach that his lucky dog tie had already let him down. If the dogs were bringing him luck tonight, it was *bad* luck. That streak of red he saw scuttling toward his car was Dana.

Now I'm stuck, he realized with a groan.

Although Tom looked devastatingly handsome as he strode across the parking lot, Dana frowned. She'd come early expecting a few minutes alone at his car to carry out her plan, but now his arrival had spoiled everything.

Now what am I supposed to do? Dana fumed.

128

Desperately she tried to come up with a revised plan.

Stall, she told herself. She slipped the strap of her crochet bag over her shoulder to free her hand and waved as he approached. "Hi, honey bunch," she said, leaning against the front fender of his blue Saturn and blocking his way to the driver's-side door. "You look scrumptious tonight. We don't need to go to Bruce's old dinner party if you don't want to. Let's just stay here and—"

"I'm going to this party, Dana. And nothing you say or do is going to stop me."

Wanna bet? she longed to say, but she simply smiled mysteriously and struck a seductive pose. "Aren't you going to compliment me on my new dress?" She was especially proud of the bright red body-skimming jersey dress with the halter top. "I made it myself. I got the idea from an old poster of Sonny and Cher. My mom used to have all their stuff, and I've *always* loved Cher's style." She stroked Tom's arm. "I got you, babe . . . ," she sang huskily.

"Dana, just get in the car."

"How about a little hello kiss first?"

The glare he gave her undoubtedly meant no.

"Well!" she said with a pout. "Nice to see you too. I'd hoped you would be out of your bad mood by tonight, but I see you're still in a snit!" Still blocking his way to the driver's-side door, she backed up and ducked her head to look into the side-view mirror. "Well, no wonder you don't want to kiss me. My lips are totally pale and dry!"

She dug around in her bag and pulled out a tube of lipstick. Leaning over the mirror again, she slowly and carefully applied a thick, dark red coat. "Now. Isn't that better?" she asked, puckering her lips. "Hmmm . . . no? Well, maybe one more coat." She bent and painstakingly applied a second layer. "Perfect," she said, straightening up.

With her eyes locked on Tom's, she tried to tuck the lipstick back into her purse but missed. It hit the concrete parking lot with a clink and rolled away.

"Oh no! That's my favorite color! Don't worry. I'll get it." She leaned over to retrieve the rolling tube. As she grabbed for it she toed it slightly to make it roll farther away. Finally she snatched it up. "I hope it's not damaged. I'd better check." Knowing full well that she was making Tom furious, she opened the tube and slowly twisted the lipstick out to its full position to examine it.

Suddenly Tom's hands were on her bare shoulders. It wasn't a gentle I-want-you touch; it was a get-out-of-my-way grab—exactly the reaction Dana had counted on. Letting out a feigned squeak and stumbling in her red platform shoes, she crashed into Tom, the open lipstick still in her hand.

"Dana! You—how could you be so—" Tom jumped back and glared at her. "Look what you've done!"

Dana fought back a triumphant grin as she saw the smear of red lipstick across his tie and shirt. "Oops! Clumsy me. Sorry!"

"Now I'll have to go change again!" He started away but turned back suddenly. "And *don't* follow me!" Head down and arms swinging, Tom raged all the way back to the dorm.

"Don't worry. I'll stay *right here*," she said calmly after he'd gone. She hated messing up his clothes, especially when he looked so handsome and sexy, but one stalling technique was as good as another. "Besides, you don't *really* want to go to that party and see Elizabeth Wakefield, Tom," she whispered. "You might think you do, but I know what's best for you. And that's for you to stay here with me."

Dana strolled casually to the rear of the car, and yet her calmness was only on the surface. Inside she was as agitated as a load of laundry. Her heart was pounding dangerously and her hands were sweaty.

At least she could be grateful for the way Tom had parked. By backing into the parking space with the car's rear against the concrete wall, he'd never see her handiwork until it was too late.

Dana glanced around nervously. Convinced the coast was clear, she hiked up her tight dress, and with calculated accuracy she kicked at the right taillight. A jarring pain shot up her leg, but the taillight remained intact. Again she kicked . . . and again. Finally the red plastic cracked. She kicked it once more for good measure. Whistling nonchalantly, she moved to the left light and repeated the action.

"Let's see if you make it to that party now," she murmured, glancing toward the dorm. She quickly smoothed her dress back into place and brushed the red plastic chips off her shoes. Then with a deep, calming breath she hurried around to the passenger-side door and climbed inside. The adrenaline that had earlier been pumped into her body now surged around with no outlet, making her feel jittery and weak. She laid her head back against the headrest and waited for her heartbeat to slow to a more normal pace.

When she felt once more in control, she sat forward and twisted the rearview mirror in her direction. Taking a Kleenex out of her bag, she wiped off her excess lipstick and tucked a few curly strands of dark hair back into her French twist, but it didn't help her appearance much. Her face was flushed and shiny with perspiration.

"You look like a criminal," she scolded her reflection. "Dana, face it. You are a *very* bad girl! That was the *stupidest* thing you've *ever* done!"

She flopped back against the headrest and shut her eyes. Instead of relaxing darkness she saw visions of Tom sinking naively into Elizabeth Wakefield's clutches. "No," she gasped, opening her eyes to chase away the image. "I had to do it. I *had* to. I'm desperate. I care about Tom too much to lose him now."

She looked in the direction of Reid Hall and whispered, "Forgive me, Tom, but I had to do it . . . for your own good."

Although Elizabeth had been in the Patmans' house many times before, she'd rarely been in the lounge off the dining area. Tonight she felt very privileged and grown-up. In fact, the way people had been coming up to her and congratulating her about her acceptance to DCIR, she felt as if she were the guest of honor.

Leaving Scott in the hands of Bruce for a while, she walked over to a small table and picked up a canapé. She'd have never believed that crazy Winston Egbert would have culinary talents. But then, it seemed as if Winston had developed a lot of new talents since he'd been dating Denise. Elizabeth smiled at the thought of how her old friend had matured since he'd found his true love.

At least *someone's* college romance was working out.

Elizabeth looked around the room. It was a strange blend of elegance and casualness—a very Patman combination. Above her head was a row of professionally framed Patman-family photos. Most of them were shots of Bruce with tennis trophies. But a few were of Bruce and his airplane, Bruce with his race car, and just Bruce. No one could ever accuse the Patmans of ignoring their only son.

She smiled as Scott waved and winked flirtatiously at her from across the room. He looked exceptionally handsome tonight in his dark blue suit—very self-assured, as if he were in his true element.

"Elizabeth, you look marvelous," Lila said.

"Thanks, Lila. You look great too." Lila's off-the-shoulder, royal blue cocktail dress made her look like a supermodel. But Lila always looked impeccable.

With her money she could afford to look perfect every hour, every day.

"I love that white suit. *Très* chic," she said.

"Thanks." Elizabeth didn't mention that Scott had picked it out or that she'd spent half the afternoon trying to iron the wrinkles out of it. Which reminded her . . .

"Lila, have you seen Jessica?" So far her sister hadn't put in an appearance at the party. In fact, Elizabeth hadn't seen her since she'd stormed out of their dorm room earlier that afternoon.

"Jessica was at my apartment all afternoon. She wanted to borrow a dress from me for tonight, and then she selected the most *awful* thing! My black satin shirtdress. I told her it looked like funeral attire, but she said it fit her mood. I tried and tried to talk her out of it, but you know Jess—when she makes up her mind, you might as well back away and let her go with it."

Elizabeth nodded her understanding. She knew better than anyone how stubborn Jessica could be, and that didn't stop the sinking feeling in her stomach any.

"Of course Jessica would look gorgeous in any ol' thing." Lila patted Elizabeth's arm comfortingly. "Don't worry. Nick picked her up around six. I'm sure they'll be here soon."

Morris, the Patmans' butler, walked past them with a tray of champagne-filled glasses. Lila reached out and snagged one. "See, I *told* you they'd break out the best bubbly to celebrate your news."

Elizabeth smiled but was saved from further comment by Scott. He slipped one arm around her waist and the other around Lila's.

"Lila," he gushed. "Great party. You look fabulous, by the way."

As Lila batted her eyelashes and basked in his compliments he tightened his grip on Elizabeth. "I hope you'll excuse us," he crooned to Lila, "but I have someone important I want Liz to meet."

Elizabeth tottered slightly on her high heels as he tugged her away from Lila and dragged her across the room. She shouldn't have been surprised, however. He'd been doing it all night.

"This is Gregory Razer," Scott said, introducing her to a tall, athletic-looking man in his early thirties. "He's publisher of *West Words Weekly*."

Elizabeth had never heard of the publication, but she smiled politely. Scott seemed to know so many people in the journalism field.

"Gregory says they always have openings for eager young journalists willing to learn the magazine game. I told him you'd probably be interested in part-time work when we get to Denver."

Elizabeth's eyes opened wide, and she attempted to cover her surprise with a polite smile and nod. *Just wait till I get you alone!* she thought, cutting a glance at Scott. *What makes you think you're an authority on what I want?*

"Oh, and here's Bill Wilson," Scott said nonchalantly. "He and my father used to be business partners, but now Bill's the head of Globe Net Multinational."

"Really?" Elizabeth said politely as the man grasped her hand. "That's one of the largest media conglomerates in the nation, isn't it?"

"In the *world*," Scott corrected.

Bill Wilson was an extremely tall man with a thick bushy mustache and dark curly hair. He beamed down at her. "You must be Scott's little girlfriend! So you want to be a journalist, eh? I've heard a lot about you."

Apparently from the NEWS2US *article,* she thought, flushing with anger at his patronizing tone.

Scott seemed to sense her discomfort and stepped forward. "Globe Net's corporate headquarters are in Denver."

"And I hear you two are soon to be my neighbors," Bill added.

Lucky us, Elizabeth thought sarcastically, but as Bill continued to talk about his family and his job she wondered if she had been too rash. She didn't like to make snap judgments about people. He seemed friendly enough. Elizabeth decided to let the "little girlfriend" crack slide for now.

Bill patted her arm. "Patsy and I fully expect you two to be our frequent guests while you're attending DCIR. We have a home in Denver and a condo in Aspen. Have you ever skied in the Rockies? I know Scott loves to ski. The two of you must come some weekend. I insist."

"We'd love to," Scott gushed, completely ignoring the look of amazement Elizabeth shot at him.

"Great. Just let me know when, and I'll send my helicopter for you."

Helicopter? It sounded like fun, but Elizabeth couldn't believe how Scott accepted the invitation without so much as a glance in her direction. *I wouldn't mind being consulted occasionally about my future,* she thought. *Well, he seems to know all the right people and just what to say to them. Maybe I'd better just keep my mouth shut.*

Elizabeth smiled when she saw Winston waving from the kitchen door. "Excuse me," she said as she headed toward him.

Scott followed her. "Where are you going?" he asked.

"To the kitchen. I thought I'd just pop in and say hello to Winston and Denise."

"Really, Elizabeth, I don't think you should. How would it look?"

"It'd look like I was saying hello to my friends," she said indignantly.

He caught her arm at the elbow. "There are a lot of important people here. You really ought to be using this time more wisely. Make some connections of your own, at least. I can't do everything for you."

"You could have fooled me," she mumbled under her breath.

Chapter Eight

This yellow shirt doesn't match my khakis, Tom thought gloomily as he drove toward the Patmans' mansion. *And this striped tie is all wrong. Elizabeth will think I dressed in the dark. And now I'm going to be late. That'll* really *impress her.*

The Saturn leaped forward as Tom furiously mashed his foot against the accelerator. He hardly glanced at the speedometer. He knew he was speeding, but at this point he was way beyond caring. *Well, at least I'm not covered in mud with rain streaming down my face.* He cringed, remembering Elizabeth's look of horror when she'd seen him earlier that afternoon. *That has to rank as one of the five worst moments of my life.*

". . . and then Anthony threw all the music up in the air and yelled at the violinists for the next fifteen minutes. . . ."

Tom gritted his teeth as Dana's chattering wore down his already thin nerves.

". . . I knew my part *flawlessly,* but being in the orchestra is like playing sports, you know; teamwork and all that. And *then* when I finally got home, Felicity—you know, my housemate? Well, she hogged the bathroom *forever.* I had to dress and get back to campus in such a rush, it's a wonder I made it at all. . . ."

Tom figured she was waiting for him to make a comment. He didn't.

"I was afraid if I didn't show up on time, you'd feel like I'd stood you up or something," she continued breathlessly. "As grumpy as you've been lately, I didn't want take any chances." She pouted prettily and leaned over the console between the seats. "Aren't you glad I showed up on time?"

He clamped his jaw shut and pressed harder on the accelerator.

"Tom?"

He could smell her citrusy perfume and was certain her clingy dress was meant to distract him, but he kept his attention on the road. He was driving way too fast to get involved in Dana's antics now.

"I knew you'd like this dress," she purred, smoothing the clingy knit material across her thighs. "Didn't you tell me once that red was your favorite color?" She leaned in his direction and lowered her voice. "Elizabeth never wore red for you, did she?"

For some reason the idea that Dana would dare

139

utter Elizabeth's name made his blood boil. "Elizabeth preferred more subdued colors," he said through clenched teeth. He didn't realize that his foot had pressed harder against the accelerator until he heard the engine roar in protest.

Tom reached back and kneaded his tense neck muscles. *Relax,* he told himself. But he couldn't obey. He could feel a throbbing at the base of his skull that signaled the beginning of a major tension headache.

Suddenly he heard the wail of sirens. With a sinking feeling in the pit of his stomach he glanced into the rearview mirror. Just as he'd feared, the blue and red flashing lights of a police car reflected back at him.

Dana sank back into the seat and covered her grin with her hand. This was working out even better than she'd hoped. She hadn't planned on Tom's speeding; it was just the icing on the cake. Once again his hot temper had worked *against* him and *for* her. If she'd known Tom was going to speed like a maniac, she could have left the taillights alone. He was bound to get pulled over sometime. *One traffic violation is as good as another,* she thought. *And two are twice as good!*

Tom rolled down his window and sat muttering to himself as the policeman approached.

"Do you know how fast you were driving?" the policeman asked.

Tom sat stiffly with his hands on the steering wheel. "Not exactly."

"I clocked you at thirty miles an hour over the posted speed limit." The officer pushed his hat back from his face. "Can I see your license and registration, please."

Dana stifled a giggle as Tom reached across her and snatched a handful of papers from the glove compartment. He handed them to the officer without a word before fishing his license from his wallet.

"Speeding is a dangerous habit. Especially this time of the evening and when the roads are still wet from today's rain. You should—"

"Yes, I know," Tom said in an unnatural voice. "I'm very sorry, but I *am* in a hurry. Could you possibly skip the lecture and just write out the ticket and let us be on our way?"

The officer looked at Tom, then across at Dana. "You two are all dressed up," he observed politely as he copied information from Tom's license. "It must be some important party for you to be in this big a rush."

Dana couldn't believe how civil the policeman was being. Not when Tom was stewing like a volcano about ready to blow.

"One other thing I might mention—"

"Just give me the ticket!" Tom snapped.

Dana's eyes went wide with surprise, but the officer maintained his cool exterior. He simply leaned closer into the car and looked across at Dana and then back at Tom. "I'll be happy to oblige," he said before lapsing into silence.

The policeman flipped a sheet on his pad and scribbled a moment longer before passing the pad through the window to Tom. "Sign here, please."

Tom scribbled his name.

"And here."

After Tom signed, the officer ripped the tickets from his book. "This ticket is for speeding," he declared, handing the ripped copy through the window. "And this one is for driving with no taillights."

"What? My taillights are—"

Dana accidently let out a nervous snicker.

It wasn't loud, but Tom must have heard. He turned toward her, his handsome features contorted with rage. "What do you know about this?"

She lifted her palms and shoulders innocently.

Tom slammed his hands against the steering wheel. Dana winced and shrank back into her seat—a movement not missed by the cop.

"You *knew,* didn't you?" Tom hissed. "Why didn't you tell me, Dana? Why? Oh, I get it. You wanted me to get stopped, that's why. You wanted me to miss this party, didn't you? You—you . . ." Again Tom slammed the palms of his hands against the steering wheel. The horn beeped in protest.

The officer scowled and stepped back. "Son, would you step out of the car, please."

"What? No. I—"

"Out of the car, son. And keep your hands where I can see them." The officer crouched slightly so his eyes could meet Dana's. "Don't worry, miss. Everything is going to be all right," he said reassuringly.

"I hope so," Dana whispered weakly. She

crossed her arms across her chest and shrank back into the seat. Unable to watch what was going on outside the car, she squeezed her eyes tightly shut. *I've gone too far this time,* she thought remorsefully. *Things have really gotten* way *out of control.*

Bored and annoyed, Jessica sat on a puffy white leather love seat, jiggling the ice in her glass of diet soda. Nick had hardly spoken to her since they'd arrived at the Patmans' house. He was too busy "mingling," as he called it. Until tonight Jessica had never heard him use the word *mingling.* Quite frankly, she hoped she'd never hear him use it again.

She glared across the room to where he casually leaned against the baby grand piano, talking to a bunch of guys who looked like Lawyer Ken dolls. With their pastel shirts, their button-down collars, and their bright power ties, they all appeared as if they'd been stamped from the same mold. And Nick, in his new suit, fit right in.

Where'd he get that outfit anyway? Jessica wondered. *Central casting for lawyers?*

"Smile," Lila said, joining her.

"Just look at him over there," Jessica grumbled.

Lila spun around. "Who?"

"Nick. Can you believe the way he's dressed?"

"I know. That new image he's got going is positively dreamy—not that he wasn't absolutely gorgeous before, Jess."

Jessica rolled her eyes. "Doesn't he remind you of anyone?"

Lila stared at Nick, her finger tapping her lips. "Yes, now that you mention it. He resembles that cute guy in that new lawyer movie. Oh, what's it called? You know, the one based on that John Grisham book."

Jessica shook her head. "No. He looks just like my *brother*."

"Steven? Hmmm . . . I guess he does, in a way. But there's nothing wrong with that. I've always thought your older brother was way more handsome than you give him credit for."

"Yeah, he's *cute* enough but about as dull as a movie with subtitles."

Bruce Patman walked up and whispered something in Lila's ear. She giggled and whispered in his.

Jessica sighed with disgust. Of *course* Lila would think Nick looked fantastic. Just consider what she had to compare him to—Bruce Patman, the absolute king of the preppies. And tonight Nick was vying to be prince.

They all *look alike*, Jessica thought. *Bruce; Mr. Patman; my brother, Steven; my dad; and now Nick! Dull, duller, dullest.* She glanced past Lila and Bruce to where Nick was laughing and gesturing up a storm. *That face is still heart-stoppingly gorgeous, and he's got muscles even the stuffiest jacket can't hide. But what good is that if he's* dull?

"Excuse us, Jess," Bruce said politely. "There's

someone over here I want Lila to meet."

Sure, leave me, Jessica thought as they moved away. *You might as well. Everyone else is. Elizabeth is literally moving a thousand miles away; Nick is figuratively moving a million.*

Jessica looked around the room for her sister. Elizabeth wasn't hard to spot in her tailored white suit. She was dressed for the lawyers' corner too, but that wasn't unusual. Elizabeth had originated the dress-for-boring-success look. Jessica waved, but before Elizabeth could respond, Scott Sinclair dragged her across the room again. All evening he'd been lording her around like a diamond he'd acquired at an estate sale.

Would this party never end?

One of Bruce's fraternity brothers leaned into view. "Hi. Aren't you Jessica Wakefield?" he asked. "We have a mutual friend—Magda Helperin. You're both Thetas, right?"

Jessica gazed into eyes as deep as the ocean and twice as blue. He was cute, in a cowboy sort of way. She'd seen him at a party or two, but she couldn't remember his name.

"Trent. Trent Goodman. I heard all about what happened to you at the country club. Undercover police work must be incredibly exciting. Did you really save your sister's life?"

"Mm-hmm." Jessica nodded and glanced across the room to see if Nick had noticed she was talking to a cute guy. He hadn't. He looked as if he had been hypnotized by the power stripes on Mr. Patman's tie.

"You aren't working undercover now, are you?" When he didn't get a response, Trent leaned closer. "I mean, you're not going to whip out a badge and start carding us or something?"

Jessica smiled weakly. "No. I'm off duty." She looked again at Nick. *Couldn't he at least get a teeny bit jealous?* she stewed.

"Is anyone sitting here?" Trent gestured to the empty space on the love seat.

Jessica's anger at Nick stuck in her throat. "It doesn't *look* like it, does it?"

Trent backed away slightly. "Oh—sorry. Maybe you'd rather be alone."

"No offense, but I think I would."

"I won't bother you, then. Maybe we'll talk sometime when you're feeling better."

Jessica chewed her bottom lip and watched the Sigma walk away. *Isn't it odd how a perfect stranger would notice how I feel when Nick hasn't noticed a thing?* she wondered. *What's happened between us? Worse, what's going to? This new Nick is not the same person I fell in love with.*

Jessica propped her elbow on the arm of the love seat and rested her chin in the palm of her hand. *How could my life possibly get any worse?* she wondered.

"You're crazy, you know that?" Denise declared as she watched Winston make faces at his reflection in the bottom of a gleaming copper pan. Even as nervous and frazzled as she was, Winston could always make her laugh.

"*Moi?*" he kidded, pushing the tall white chef's hat out of his eyes.

"*Oui, toi.*" She wagged a finger at the long matching apron that came down almost to his ankles. "I don't know how anyone can get so messy simply arranging food. From looking at you, no one could tell that *I* did all the real cooking." She handed him a rag. "You even have flour on your glasses. How did that get there?"

Winston shrugged, removed his glasses, and gave them a swipe with the rag.

"Here," Denise ordered. "Make yourself useful. Put two of these carrot curls on top of each salad."

Winston bowed deeply. "You command, oh mighty chef, and I obey."

Denise popped a tray of croissants into the double-wide stainless steel oven. "I hope these turn out as flaky as the last ones I made." She turned around in a circle. "Where's the honey butter? You didn't melt it in with the sauce for the lobster, did you?"

"It's here somewhere," Winston said. "Quit worrying so much."

"I can't help it. You know what this dinner means to me."

Winston dished out a clump of salad and poked at it with a fork. "Don't you think these tomatoes are slightly underripe?"

"*Now* who's worrying?"

"Well, they look like they're just starting to turn red."

"They're supposed to be that color. They're called orange blush."

"Tomatoes are supposed to be red."

"And lobster is supposed to be lobster, not tofú. But that hasn't stopped us, has it?"

"Denise!" Winston scolded. "Quit worrying about it. Bruce loved the lobster *al* Denise, and so will everybody else here tonight."

"Quit telling me not to worry. I'll worry if I want to. I worried all morning, I worried all afternoon, and I'll be worried tonight until every crumb of food is gone and we've got a check in our hands." Denise double-checked the temperature setting on the oven. "Do you think everyone is here yet? I'm ready to get this show on the road. The sooner we serve, the sooner this will all be over."

"It shouldn't be long now. Last time I looked out, there were a lot of people here. Mostly people I didn't know, but I saw Elizabeth and Scott, Bruce and Lila, and Jessica and Nick."

"I thought Jessica would pop in here and say hello, didn't you?"

"She didn't look like she was having much fun. She's dressed all in black like she's in mourning. And you should see Nick. He looks like he's joined the Young Republicans."

"*This* I've *got* to see." Denise tiptoed to the

148

door and peeked into the Patmans' drawing room like a nervous actress peeking through the stage curtains before a show. She didn't see Nick, but . . . no, it couldn't be . . . the orangy tan, the over-coiffed hair . . .

"Oh no!" Denise cried, slamming the door. "We're sunk!"

"What now?" Winston said. "You've been having one crisis after another all day. I'll be glad when we quit the catering business and go back to being regular students."

"It's Hal Horner! Nobody told me *he* was going to be here."

Winston dropped his voice an octave and puffed out his chest. "'If you've been hornswoggled, call Hal Horner'—*that* Hal Horner?"

"The very same. We're dead meat."

"Don't jump the gun, Denise. I'm sure he's here as a guest, not to investigate us."

"What does it matter," Denise moaned. "The minute we serve our infamous fake lobster, Mrs. Patman is going to scream, 'I've been hornswoggled!' and Hal will crank up his video camera. He's *ruthless*, Winnie. I've seen him work. Together they'll have Nick arrest us, and we'll be hauled off to jail. And do you think we'll be able to make bail? Not with my credit record!" She sank onto a chair and put a hand over her heart. "I can just see us now on tomorrow's newscast."

Winston fanned Denise with a cookie sheet.

149

"Quit gasping like that. You're going to hyper-ventilate!"

Denise jerked the pan from his hand and jumped into his arms. "I don't want to go to jail!"

The moment Winston wrapped his arms comfortingly around her, Denise heard the swinging door and the clip-clop of Mrs. Patman's heels on the tile floor.

"Am I interrupting you two again?" Mrs. Patman asked, lifting her delicately shaped eyebrows. "Well, I'll be quick. I came to tell you that Morris is seating the guests now. You can serve the food . . . if you're ready," she finished doubtfully.

Denise gulped. "Everything is ready, Mrs. Patman. The food will be right out."

When Mrs. Patman left, Denise slumped against the refrigerator door.

"So what are we going to do?" Winston asked.

"Run away?"

Winston saluted good-naturedly. "I'll go start up the Bug."

"No. Wait!" She grabbed him by the apron strings and jerked him to a stop. "We can't do that. We've still got all this food to pay for."

Winston stood at attention like a soldier awaiting orders.

"Stall," she whispered hoarsely. "We'll just have to kill time until I can think of what to do." She shoved a tray at him. "Here. We'll serve in courses. You take out the salads while I check on the rolls."

150

He took two steps before she yanked him to a stop again.

"Wait. Dump more croutons on each salad. Maybe we can fill everyone up before they get to the main course."

Tom could feel a breeze each time another car whipped past him, but it wasn't cooling his temper any. "You don't have any right to treat me like a criminal," he argued.

"Put your hands back on the car, please," the policeman said before continuing to pat Tom down.

Tom gritted his teeth. With every slap of the man's hands against his clothing he was reminded that Elizabeth was slipping further away. "Listen," Tom continued. "I admit I was speeding, and I'm perfectly willing to pay the fine."

"Thirty miles an hour over the posted—"

"I know. I know. You told me. But I didn't know that I was going *that* fast. It was an honest mistake. People do make mistakes, you know. And as for my taillights, they were fine before we left the dorm. They've been deliberately broken; any fool can see that."

The policeman tugged his shoulder, which Tom took as an indication that he was finally able to turn and face him.

"Will you touch the tip of your finger to the end of your nose for me, please."

151

Tom sucked in an irritated breath and practically punched himself in the nose. "I haven't been drinking, Officer."

"Can you stand on one foot, please?"

Tom shook his head. "No. I have an important dinner party to get to. I don't have time for gymnastics here on the side of the road!"

"Then I'm afraid you'll have to take a Breathalyzer test."

"I'm not taking any test of any kind," he shouted. "I know my rights! This is harassment. I demand you let me go. I've signed the stupid ticket and—"

"Son, I'm not about to let you get back in that car and drive away when I feel other motorists could be in danger—not to mention your girlfriend."

"She's *not* my girlfriend," Tom growled through clenched teeth. "Not anymore."

The policeman's eyebrows wrinkled until they formed an almost solid line across his forehead. "Well, I'm worried about the young lady."

"Dana's not in any danger—not from me. I've never laid a hand on her. You can ask her if you don't believe me."

"Son, I suggest you come on back to my car—"

"Why don't you just leave me alone? Go catch some real criminals." Tom grabbed for his door handle.

The officer reached for his handcuffs. "Am I going to have to arrest you?"

"Take a hike!"

152

Tom suddenly felt his neck being grabbed and his head pushed roughly against the Saturn. "Put your hands behind your back!" he heard the policeman bark. As he felt the cold metal of handcuffs snapping around his wrists Tom laid his head on top of the car and wished he were dead.

"Winston! Don't eat those!" Denise wailed, snatching the jar of maraschino cherries from his sticky fingers. "Here, arrange these melon balls in those sherbet glasses. Oh, great! Where are those pineapple cubes?"

"Come off the manic panic, Denise. Everything is going fine."

"I can't help it. We're in big trouble here. I just know it. I'm never going to get my credit cards paid off. I'll lose my scholarship. I'll be the first person in my family to flunk out of college—"

"Don't forget the part about being the first person in your family to go to jail."

Denise glared at Winston until he grinned.

"Get a grip, sweetie. They liked the salad, didn't they? Especially after you wowed them with the crescent rolls and the honey butter?"

"Yes, but . . ." She jumped back as steam billowed from the large pot of soup she'd just uncovered. "Here," she said. "You ladle, I'll garnish."

"Gag. What *is* this stuff?" Winston asked, gazing into the pot with a pained expression.

"Shiitake bisque."

"What?"

"Shiitake—oh . . . *mushrooms,* you dope. Cream of mushroom soup."

Winston shook his head. "Glad I'm not rich."

As if on cue, Mrs. Patman poked her head in the door. "Yoo-hoo! Denise, dear, is there a problem? Everyone finished their salads quite a while ago."

"Sorry, Mrs. Patman," Denise called back as sweetly as her tensed vocal cords would allow. "We're on our way with the soup course now."

Distracted middip, Winston missed the china bowl he was aiming for and dumped a ladleful of soup onto the tray, drowning it in milky gray goop. "Want me to serve?" he asked, grabbing for a rag.

Denise shuddered at the very thought. She could just imagine what some of the guests would look like wearing creamed soup. As much as she adored Winston, he was not exactly known for being coordinated. "I'll do it," she insisted. "But if you'll take off that stupid hat and that dirty apron, you can take the fruit cups out and stall everyone until I can get the soup out there." She took the rag from him and dabbed at a milky stream of soup that was running down the side of the cabinet.

While Winston kept everyone occupied with the fruit, she rinsed the bowls, wiped the tray clean, and started filling them. She was dropping a mushroom and bread crumb garnish on each bowl when Winston reappeared.

154

"Mrs. Patman is right behind me," he sang under his breath as he passed her.

Again, Denise thought. *She's been in here three times in the last twenty minutes!*

"Are you sure there's no problem, dear?" Mrs. Patman asked.

"No problem. I've got the soup right here." Denise groaned slightly as she lifted the heavy tray.

"Denise, we hadn't planned for everything to dribble out of the kitchen a bite at a time. Do you think that you and Winston could coordinate just a tad better?"

"We'll try, Mrs. Patman. I guess we're both just a little nervous."

They all turned toward the door as Mr. Patman entered. "I thought you kids might get a kick out of meeting a local celebrity." He stepped aside and opened the door wider as a very cool, very arrogant Hal Horner strode into the room.

Denise gasped and set the soup on the edge of the counter to keep from spilling it.

"Soup?" Mr. Patman's disappointment was evident by his tone. "It looks delish, but when are we going to get that main course? It's Denise's own creation, Hal. You're going to *love* lobster *al* Denise. Bruce guarantees it."

"Lobster?" Hal's face suddenly went pale beneath his fake tan. "Hold everything!" he said.

Denise felt her knees wobble. *Here it comes. You're off to jail, Denise.*

"You can't serve lobster! Didn't you see my broadcast on the five o'clock news? Almost all the local stores have been sent tainted lobster. Anybody who has purchased lobster in the area today is well-advised to throw it out."

Denise didn't trust her ears. Could she be off the hook? "But—"

"Throw it out," Mrs. Patman insisted. "We can't serve it. Not now."

Denise sighed loudly with relief.

"Oh, darling, don't you worry," Mrs. Patman said, obviously misinterpreting Denise's sigh. "We'll pay you anyway. After all, it's not your fault that lobster is so easily ruined, is it?"

Mrs. Patman's high heels clicked along the quarry tile floor as she hurried to the kitchen phone. "I'll just call Gourmet Dan's Van. We order gourmet takeout from there all the time. Their Szechuan crispy duck is simply divine."

When Mrs. Patman finished her call and started out of the kitchen with Mr. Patman and Hal, Denise smiled politely. "I'll serve the soup to tide everyone over until Gourmet Dan's Van arrives," she offered.

"That'll be wonderful, dear. We'll simply have to try your famous lobster dish some other time."

As soon as the door shut behind the trio Denise jumped into Winston's arms, nearly knocking him over. "We're saved!" she squealed.

Once he recovered his balance, they began a

dance around the room that looked something like a cross between a polka and Tigger's famous bounce.

"Wasn't that a great party?" Nick asked for what must have been the tenth time since they'd gotten in the car.

Jessica closed her eyes and pretended to be asleep. It was easier that way. She didn't want talk to Nick Fox. If he didn't have time to talk to her at the Patmans', then she didn't have time to talk to him now.

"I really met a lot of interesting people tonight. And the food was great. I'm glad they didn't serve that lobster stuff. To tell you the truth, I'm not all that into it." He reached across the dark seat and fumbled for her hand, but she tucked it under the edge of her thigh.

He laid his hand on her leg. "You had a good time, didn't you, Jess?"

Despite pretending to sleep, Jessica couldn't hold back a groan. The party had been worse than dull. It'd been downright depressing. Even the food tasted like it'd come from cardboard cartons. Knowing Winston, he'd probably bought it at a take-out place and passed it off as his own special recipe.

Or maybe the food only seemed disappointing because she was already in a bad mood. Jessica had been trying to spend some time with Elizabeth all night, but she'd hardly had a chance. Every time she got within speaking distance, Scott Sinclair would drag her sister off to meet some old guy.

And Nick! She didn't even want to *think* about how he'd acted. Mr. Suit had positively ignored her.

And what'd happened to Tom Watts? She was sure he'd show up at the party. Had he simply dismissed her telephone call? Didn't he care that Elizabeth was leaving forever?

Didn't anybody care?

Chapter
Nine

OK, babe, it's time to have this out, right now. Nick whipped the Camaro into a parking space behind Dickenson Hall and clicked off the lights but made no move to get out of the car. Jessica had been pretending to be asleep all the way home. He wasn't falling for it.

"What's the problem, Jess?" Nick asked. "Come on, I know you aren't asleep. You're just ignoring me like you've been doing all night."

Her eyes flew open, and all pretense of sleepiness evaporated. "*I* ignored *you*? You've got to be joking! Did you even know I was at the party?"

"Of *course* I knew you were at the party." He relaxed somewhat and leaned toward her. It wasn't anything serious after all. Jessica was just in a snit because she hadn't gotten the lion's share of the limelight. With everyone congratulating Elizabeth and Scott, Jessica hadn't gotten the attention she craved.

"You were the most beautiful girl at the party," he said, hoping to soothe her injured feelings.

Jessica flounced in the seat and let out a huff of annoyance. "Thanks a lot!"

"I take it you didn't have fun?"

"How could I? You were horrible!"

"Me?" Nick backed away in surprise. He thought he'd done very well at the party. For once in his life he'd attended a high-society affair and didn't feel like a bull in a china shop.

Before he could come up with a reply, she turned on him. "I'm sorry, Nick, it's just not working."

His mouth suddenly felt dry and his armpits wet. "What's not working?"

"Us."

Nick stared into the sea green eyes he adored, unable to believe what he was hearing. "What do you mean? Are you telling me you want to break up?"

She nodded.

Oh no, he thought. *Please let this be one of Jessica's little bids for attention.* He searched her face for any clue—a tear, a grin, a pout. Nothing. "You don't mean that." Nick reached for her hand.

Jessica pulled it away.

"I thought you loved me," he said in a pathetically weak voice.

"I do, or I did, but—"

Nick's heart had stopped beating. "But what?"

"I loved Nick the cop, not Nick the future lawyer. You've changed."

"Everybody changes."

"Why? Why change when things are fine just the way they are?"

"They weren't fine. That's just it," he said. "I want something better for us than a cop's life." He'd known all along that Jessica wasn't one hundred percent for his leaving the police force, but until this very moment he'd thought she'd come around. "Jessica, don't you see? Every time my work put you in danger, it killed a little part of me. I had to make a change."

"OK, fine! Make your changes. And while you're at it, change relationships." She crossed her arms and stared out the windshield. "I don't think we should keep seeing each other."

How could this be happening? Jessica is the love of my life. Doesn't she realize that I'm doing it all for her? Nick squeezed his eyes shut to hold back tears.

"You'd probably be happier with someone like my sister," Jessica said.

Oh, I get it, he thought as understanding finally dawned on him. *This isn't about us. This is still about Elizabeth's leaving. Jessica isn't going to let it rest.* Anger replaced Nick's feelings of surprised hurt.

"You've got a real problem, you know that?" He yanked loose his tie and unbuttoned the top button of his dress shirt. "You don't want me to change. You don't want your sister to change. Both of us are trying to do something better for our lives. And in case you don't realize it, I'm doing all this for you."

161

Jessica let out a squeal of frustration. "I'm sick of people always doing things for my own good. Why can't anybody believe I have a mind of my own? Why can't I decide what's good for me? Nick the cop was good for me. The best thing I ever had."

Nick sighed, and his heart started to beat again. Reassured that she still loved him, he cupped her lovely face in his hands. "You're the best thing in my life too, sweetheart. But you're going to have to trust me and be patient."

She jerked away from him, but he continued to talk in as soothing a tone as he could manage. "This isn't really about us, Jess. You're just scared about Elizabeth moving away, and you're letting your fears leak out on everything else around you."

"Thank you, Joe College! I never would have understood myself without your amazing insight into my psyche."

Nick's temper flared again. "Accepting change is part of growing up, Jessica. Maybe it's time you started. Believe it or not, there *is* life beyond giggling with your sorority sisters and painting each other's fingernails." Nick couldn't stop himself now, despite the wide-eyed, stricken look on Jessica's face. "Real life is more than flirting and shopping and attending a class or two whenever you feel like it. Do you plan to be a child forever?"

As Jessica scrambled out of the car Nick leaned over her seat and shouted out the open door, "Grow up!"

* * *

Jessica slung her whole body into that door slam. The resounding bang didn't make her feel much better, however, and neither did storming up the sidewalk and stomping into Dickenson Hall's brightly lit lobby.

When her trembling knees began to give way, she leaned against the door to the stairwell. She took a deep breath and tried to get her emotions under control.

She looked at the ugly concrete steps with their nasty green metal handrails. *I'm not going up to that dumpy, depressing dorm room,* she thought. *I'm in no mood to sit there in that concrete-block cell filled with all those stupid packing crates and listen to Elizabeth blab about how exciting Denver is going to be. Why is she so happy to leave me? Why?*

Tears began to run down her cheeks. *I can't let Elizabeth see me like this. She deserves one night of peace. But where can I go? Nick's is definitely out of the question. Lila's? No, she and Bruce are staying with the Patmans for the weekend. Theta house?*

The thought brought back Nick's words, and Jessica fumed. *How dare Nick make that crack about my sorority sisters! That just shows how much he knows about sisterhood and sticking together. That's where I'll go. I'll sleep at Theta house. At least they understand me there.*

As Jessica left Dickenson Hall and headed across the dark campus her tears started to fall again. She could hear Nick's words like an echo on the wind.

"Grow up!"

I'm trying, Nick. I don't want to stay a child

163

for*ever*. She wiped her wet cheeks with the back of her hand. *But I do want to be a twin . . . and a sister forever.*

Elizabeth snapped the locks on her suitcase and slipped the little key into her purse. She looked around her half of the room—stark, barren, depressing—and sighed.

"That it?" asked Nina Harper, her best friend.

"That's it. Except for my carry-on bag, and I'll finish packing that with my essentials tomorrow morning after I get ready."

"So you're all set?"

"Well, I'm all packed. I guess it's the same thing." Elizabeth hefted the bag off her bed with a grunt and set it near the door.

Nina rattled the bag of popcorn she'd microwaved. "You're going to make me eat this whole thing by myself?"

"Never," Elizabeth assured her, plopping down on the bed beside her and grabbing a handful of kernels. She really shouldn't have been hungry, not considering all the food that had been available at the Patmans' party. But the truth was, she hadn't felt much like eating while she was there.

The popcorn's delicious aroma reminded Elizabeth of all the late nights she and Nina had put in studying. It also reminded her of the strict diet she'd been on after she'd first arrived at SVU. When depression over her breakup with Todd had caused her to overeat and put on a few pounds, it was Nina who had come to her rescue. Nina did something even more important than help her lose the weight; she'd given her sound advice and helped her regain confidence in herself. Since the day they'd met, Nina had been a true friend.

"Who's going to help me watch my diet in Denver?" she asked, grabbing another handful of popcorn.

"You'll be fine. You just went crazy that one time, and it was perfectly understandable. But if you ever find yourself hoarding chocolate chip cookies, call me. I'll talk you through it."

Elizabeth swallowed the lump in her throat. *Here's someone else I'm going to miss,* she thought.

Nina threw a kernel into the air and caught it on her tongue. "I've always wanted to do that."

Elizabeth tried it and missed. They both laughed, but it was a pretty feeble-sounding attempt. Normally they would have had a million and one things to talk about, but for several moments the only sound was the occasional crunch of popcorn being chewed.

"Nina," Elizabeth said at last. "I wish you could go to the airport with me tomorrow."

"I wish I could too, but that test in advanced physics is at nine, and I don't know how long it'll take me to finish."

"I understand." Nina was the only one of Elizabeth's friends who was as conscientious about grades as she was.

165

Again they lapsed into an uncomfortable silence. Finally Nina got up and began to putter around the room. "Is this what you're wearing tomorrow?" she asked, picking up the multicolored crinkle cotton skirt that lay draped over the back of a desk chair.

So this is what we've come to, Elizabeth thought. *Small talk—all to avoid saying good-bye.* She nodded to her friend. "I wanted something that would look nice but be comfortable."

Nina held up the vest in front of her. "I can see Jessica wearing this revealing top, but . . ." She shook her head.

"I have a light blue turtleneck to wear under it and a matching jacket to wear over it. You never know how cool it'll be on the plane."

"The layered look; that's a good idea, and blue always makes your eyes stand out." Suddenly Nina's voice broke. "We're not very good at this, are we?"

Her eyes burning, Elizabeth jumped from the bed. "Oh, Nina . . . I'm going to miss you so much," she blurted, wrapping her best friend in a desperate hug.

"Not as much as I'm going to miss you." Tears swam in Nina's big brown eyes. Seemingly embarrassed, she tried to cover her quavery voice with a throat-clearing cough. Then she sighed and tried a lighter tone. "I guess I'll be paying the library rent all alone now." It was a common joke around the dorm that Elizabeth and Nina spent so much time in the library, they had to pay rent on their own study carrels.

166

"Well, I guess Jessica could take over my spot—if you'll show her where the library is."

Nina smiled and stepped away. She wiped her eyes with the back of her hand and sniffed. "Hey, what're we blubbering about? This is a great opportunity for you. We should be happy, right?"

"I *am* happy," Elizabeth lied. "These are tears of joy, that's all."

Nina hugged her again. "Write me."

"I will," Elizabeth promised.

"And e-mail and telephone calls too."

"Plenty of them. And maybe you and Bryan could come to Denver. Scott has already planned a skiing trip for us. Maybe you could get a bunch of people together to meet us in Aspen. Wouldn't that be a great vacation?"

Listen to me, Elizabeth thought. *I haven't left yet, and already I'm trying to get all my friends to come visit me.*

Nina agreed and backed away. "I know you're tired and you have to get up early, so I'm going to leave now. But I didn't want you to get away without saying good-bye. So—" Nina held up her hands in a helpless gesture. "Good-bye, Elizabeth."

"Good-bye, Nina." Elizabeth's voice came out in a squeaky croak as she shut the door behind her friend.

With Nina gone, Elizabeth felt desperately alone. She flopped across her bed and stared at Jessica's side of the room. She'd thought her twin

167

would have been here at her side when she needed her. But no. Jessica had her own life to lead. She hadn't come home last night, and it looked as if she wasn't coming home tonight either. It was Elizabeth's last night, and she was all alone.

True, since Elizabeth had gotten home from the Patmans' party, she'd had a few visitors and phone calls. Besides Nina, Alexandra Rollins, her old friend from high school, had stopped by to wish her good luck. And she'd gotten calls from her brother, Steven, and her parents. Even Todd had called. But it was funny, she could have gotten calls from half the kids on campus and it wouldn't have made up for the calls she *didn't* get. She stared at the phone as if it were that traitorous piece of technology's fault that she hadn't heard from Tom. *I'm being ridiculous,* she thought. *He doesn't even know I'm leaving tomorrow. Why would he call?*

She threw a pillow across to Jessica's side of the room. "Where are you, Jessica? *I'd* be here if *you* were leaving tomorrow." Abandoned by her own sister! She was probably off with Nick somewhere, and had forgotten all about her.

Elizabeth reached up and clicked off the light. All around her she could hear the sounds of the dorm: doors slamming, radios and TVs playing, a shower running, people laughing and shouting. Somewhere overhead a chair scraped across the floor. She wasn't alone, and yet she was. Terribly, terribly alone.

I know I'll have to get used to living by myself, she thought. *But I'm not used to it now.*

She pulled up the covers and closed her eyes. *The only good thing about being alone is that I can cry as hard and loud as I want without bothering anyone.* And as if to prove her point, she did.

Chapter Ten

"What? Who? Just a minute." Nick rubbed his eyes, cleared his throat, and sat up in bed. *Is it morning?* he wondered. After worrying about Jessica for half the night, he felt as if he'd just fallen asleep. He tried to focus on the glowing numbers of the alarm clock. *That can't be right,* he thought. *Who'd be calling at five* A.M.? He put the phone back to his ear. "Hello?"

"Nick, it's me, Bill Fagen. Down at the precinct. Did I wake you?"

"Uh-huh," Nick mumbled. He was still not quite awake.

"Of course I did," Bill said with a chuckle. "No more working man's hours for you, right?"

"Right," Nick said with a yawn.

"Listen. I really didn't want to call this early, but there's some dude down here in the holding cell named Tom Watts. He claims he's a friend of yours."

"Tom? In jail?" Not only did those words wake him, but they nearly put him in shock. "Tom *Watts*? Are you sure?"

"Tom Watts. Yeah, that's the name he said."

"What happened?" Nick asked, blinking away the last of his blurriness.

"I don't know. Officer Fultz on traffic duty brought him in sometime last night. The report isn't very clear. I don't know if it's domestic violence or traffic violations. There was definitely a speeding ticket and . . . uh-oh, this isn't too good . . . driving without taillights . . . possible DUI . . . resisting arrest. . . . There's a long list here."

Nick couldn't believe his ears. "I'm on my way," he shouted. And he was already stepping into his jeans before Bill hung up the phone.

By the time Nick had his Camaro out on the highway, he was wide awake, but his head was still reeling. *What's going on?* he thought. *Jessica fighting with me over nothing . . . Elizabeth taking off for Denver on the spur of the moment . . . Tom Watts, one of the most responsible and upstanding guys in Sweet Valley, in jail? Is everyone going crazy?*

In front of the Sweet Valley police station Nick pulled into a "detectives only" spot—forgetting for a moment that he was no longer employed by the SVPD. "Old habits die hard," he said as he strode across the familiar sidewalk.

The bright morning sun was glinting off the huge glass-and-stone-fronted building. Despite its

171

size and purpose the precinct house seemed homey and welcoming to him, but he was certain Tom would be feeling otherwise by now.

Pushing his sunglasses to the top of his head, he hurried inside. He rushed through the reception area, waving amiably at the familiar faces who called out to him. It felt nice to be home—*back*, that is. But Nick knew he was beyond this now.

At least he still had enough pull around the place to get Tom sprung with a minimum of hassle. After a call to Officer Fultz and a short meeting with Chief Wallace, Nick had Tom released to his custody in less than twenty-five minutes.

"You've got to drive me to campus," Tom insisted as they walked toward the Camaro.

Nicked looked into Tom's sleep-deprived, bloodshot eyes. "Did you think I was just going to leave you out here on the sidewalk?"

"No." Tom rubbed a hand over his unshaven chin. "I mean, I've got to get to Elizabeth's dorm. Drive me to Dickenson, OK?"

"C'mon, man. You don't want to go see Elizabeth looking like this, do you?" Tom looked as bad as some of the worst drunks Nick had ever thrown in the can, but his appearance was only half the problem. Nick didn't have the heart to tell Tom that Elizabeth was probably already gone by now. Since Tom had spent the night in jail, he probably hadn't heard about Elizabeth's revised plans. "Tom, Elizabeth is leaving for Denver this morning."

Tom looked at his watch. "I know. That's why I have to get there . . . now."

Nick recognized the look on Tom's face. He'd seen it in his own mirror last night when it sank in that he might have lost Jessica forever. Today he could totally sympathize with the pain of a man in love.

"Hop in," he said.

Elizabeth had stripped the sheets and blankets from her bed, packed them, and taped shut the last packing box. All her belongings now sat in tall cartons waiting to be picked up by the freight company. Plopping down on the bare mattress, she folded her hands in her lap and waited to be picked up too.

She looked at Jessica's side of the room: the lived-in side. Jessica's bed was always a jumble of clothing, magazines, pillows, and blankets, but this morning it had a mockingly unslept-in look. Once again her sister hadn't come home.

My own twin doesn't even care that I'm leaving, Elizabeth thought sadly. *This is it—our first big separation and she's . . . she's forgotten about me already.* Tears welled in Elizabeth's eyes.

She rushed to the sink. Wetting the corner of a towel, she dabbed away her tears. "You knew this day would come," she scolded her mournful-looking reflection. But her reflection only burst into tears again and wailed back at her, "Yes, but I didn't know it would be this painful!"

For the second time that morning she picked up

173

the phone and dialed half of Nick's number before hanging up. There had to be some way to contact Jessica. But what if she hadn't stayed at Nick's? From the look of things at the Patmans' party, they weren't exactly getting along like they used to.

Elizabeth couldn't bear the thought of leaving without smoothing things over with Jessica. If phoning was out of the question, she'd leave a note. She dug a notepad from her purse and tore out a slip of pink paper, but for once in her life her writing skills failed her. There were no words in her vocabulary adequate enough to tell her sister how much she'd miss her. Besides, Jessica was going to show up . . . any minute now. Right?

Since the paper was already in her hand, she quickly jotted down her flight information. *Just in case,* she thought.

Note in hand, she looked at Jessica's bulletin board. A note there would be swallowed up in the layers of "important stuff" Jessica hadn't cleaned off since coming to SVU. She yanked out a tack, sending a shower of pictures and papers raining down on Jessica's already messy bed, and stuck the note on her own bare corkboard.

That done, Elizabeth began to pace. "What have I forgotten?" she mumbled. "Something's not right." She felt as if she should be doing something, but what? Scott had already done everything.

She shook her wrist and held her watch to her ear to see if it was still ticking. It was. Fidgeting, she took out the travel brochure about Denver and looked at it for the hundredth time. Tossing it aside, she sighed. She was going to have to do something to keep her mind occupied or she'd go stark raving mad. With a sigh of exasperation she pulled the scrunchie from her ponytail and set about fixing her hair in a French braid. She was standing before the mirror when someone knocked.

"Jessica!" she shouted with relief. "It's about time you got here. Did you forget your key?"

When she jerked open the door, the smile fell from her face. It was Scott—thirty minutes early. His sun-streaked hair fell over his eyes and he looked frazzled, as if he'd dressed hurriedly.

"Are you ready?" he said breathlessly.

"I think so." She smiled, hoping to cover for her previous expression of disappointment. "Is something wrong? You're awfully early."

He stepped into the room. "Well, as long as I was ready, I figured there was no sense just sitting around. Besides, you never know about the airport. Traffic could be bad, or weather conditions could change. It's always better to be early."

"Sure," she agreed reluctantly.

Scott looked around. "Is your sister here? I thought I heard you talking to someone."

"No . . . maybe you heard someone next door."

"Maybe." He picked up her suitcase and reached for the door. "Well, let's get going."

Elizabeth gathered her brush and hair spray and

tucked them into her leather duffel bag. She was zipping the bag shut when Scott stepped back into the room.

"I thought you said you were ready."

"I *am* ready, Scott," she assured him. She moved toward her desk.

"Well, the exit is *this* way."

She looked back over her shoulder to see if he was kidding. Strangely enough, he didn't seem to be. She sighed. "Just let me double check to make sure I'm not forgetting anything."

"If you forget something, we'll send for it. Or buy you a new one. I doubt there's anything irreplaceable in this room."

Jessica will be here any minute, she hoped. *I just know it. She wouldn't let me leave without saying good-bye.*

"Come *on,* Elizabeth. I have a cab waiting downstairs. The meter's running."

Elizabeth shouldered the duffel bag but then set it down again. "Let me check to see if I got my—"

"I've got everything we need already," Scott said impatiently. "All you need to bring is you. Come on."

Elizabeth picked up the bag and her purse and took one last look around the pale yellow room. "Scott," she said pleadingly, following him out into the hallway. "I really should wait and say good-bye to Jessica. She'll be here any minute."

"Oh, brother. You've been saying good-bye to her for two days. What about those last two parties we've been to? Hasn't that been enough hugging and crying for you? Besides, she knew you had a plane to catch. She should've been here."

"But we have plenty of time."

"No, we don't. Come on, Elizabeth." He took the duffel bag from her. "You can call your sister when we get to Denver if it's *that* important."

She stared at Scott as if he were a stranger. He certainly seemed like one. She'd never seen him act so rude and insensitive.

Scott nudged her down the stairway and practically herded her toward the cab like she was a lost sheep. Just as he was shoving her into the backseat she heard someone scream her name.

"Elizabeth, wait!" Jessica yelled, running toward the battered cab. It was happening. Her worst nightmare. Her sister really *was* leaving her—without even saying good-bye!

"I'm so sorry," she sobbed as Elizabeth climbed from the back of the cab and threw her arms around her. "I stayed at Theta house last night in Magda's room. I know I should have been with you. . . . I wanted to be, but I was just too upset to come home."

Elizabeth started to cry too. "Oh, Jessica, I'm going to miss you so much."

"Then don't go," Jessica cried, clinging to her sister. "Stay here with me where you belong. You can learn all you need to know about reporting right here at SVU."

"Jess, I *can't.*"

"I'll do anything you want, Liz. I'll clean up my

side of the room. I'll never touch your clothes without permission. I'll stay out of your business. You name it; I'll do it."

Suddenly Elizabeth was wrenched from her arms.

"C'mon, Elizabeth. Get back in the cab," Scott ordered.

He tried to wedge his way between them, but Jessica pushed him aside.

"Will you two quit acting like crybabies?" He grabbed Elizabeth's arm and practically shoved her back into the cab.

Scott Sinclair, I'd like to punch your lights out, Jessica fumed. *Why don't you go find someone else's sister to kidnap!* But suddenly Scott seemed as unimportant as last year's skirt lengths. A puff of exhaust belched from the cab, and it pulled away from the curb. Elizabeth was leaving!

Jessica ran beside the cab as it picked up speed, but it soon left her behind. "Good-bye!" she yelled, gasping for breath. "Good-bye, Elizabeth." She stood in the deserted parking lot, tears running down her cheeks, and waved until the cab was out of sight.

Even after it was gone, she stood there, unable to move, unable to feel anything. She stared at the place where the taxi had sat and tried to convince herself she wasn't dreaming. This was real.

Elizabeth was gone.

Suddenly her brain caught up to what had happened and her numbness was replaced by a wave of deep, heavy depression. Jessica had never felt so totally lost and alone. "Elizabeth is gone," she said aloud. "Now what am I going to do?"

She waited, but no answer came.

Slowly she turned toward Dickenson Hall. *I know I should be happy for Elizabeth,* she reminded herself, *but something about this feels totally wrong.*

Someone passed and gave her a funny look. *I must look awful,* she reminded herself. *Here I am wearing Magda's baggy jeans and an old Theta sweatshirt.* Her hand floated self-consciously up to her wild mane of hair. She hadn't had time to fix her hair or put on makeup, and her face was puffy from crying. *I've got to get inside before someone else sees me.*

When she reached her door, she dug her key out of the front pocket of Magda's baggy jeans. *What happens if I forget my key?* she thought. *Elizabeth won't be there anymore to let me in.*

Completely avoiding looking at Elizabeth's side, Jessica stepped into her dorm room—hers alone. No one else shared it with her now. She didn't want a room to herself. Who would she talk to? Who would help her find things she'd misplaced? Who would wake her up when she overslept? Who would be there just so she wouldn't be alone?

No one. That's who.

Maybe Nick was right, she thought gloomily. *Maybe I am being childish. Am I so afraid of change that I'm falling apart?*

She picked up a newspaper clipping from the

179

floor. "I thought this was on my bulletin board," she muttered. It was the article Elizabeth had written for the *Gazette*—the one about Jessica being a hero at Verona Springs. Jessica skimmed the article again. She'd been so proud of her undercover work and her help in solving Nick's big case. He'd been proud of her too—or so she'd thought. "Was this the action of an immature child?" she asked, showing the clipping to Nick's prominently displayed photo.

Jessica laid the clipping on her desk. *Nick was totally wrong,* she thought. *He had no right to dismiss my feelings so easily. It's natural for a person to feel sad and hurt when someone they love leaves them. Missing someone has nothing to do with growing up or being mature.*

"I *am* mature," she declared, flipping Nick's picture facedown. "You thought I was pretty mature when I saved your butt back at the chop shop bust. You thought I was all grown up the way I handled myself at the country club. But now just because I'm missing my sister, you think I'm a child. I'll show you, Nick Fox. I'll show you and everyone one else around here just how mature I really am. You think I can't handle change? Well, I'll show you change."

She began to rummage through her desk drawer. Impatiently she yanked the whole drawer out and dumped its contents onto her already crowded desktop. "I'm not afraid of change," she ranted at her reflection in the vanity mirror. "I *embrace* change. I *live* for change." She shoved the pile of junk aside and started attacking the second drawer.

"Here it is!" she shouted, holding up a tattered scrap of paper. "Sweet Valley Police Academy."

Why not? she asked herself as she dialed. *There's no reason to stay around here anymore.*

"Hello," Jessica said to the pleasant but businesslike voice that answered the phone. "I'd like some information about enrolling. . . ."

Tom skidded and nearly lost his balance as he dashed down the hallway toward room 28, Dickenson Hall. With time quickly running out, he wasn't going to give Elizabeth the opportunity to tear up his letters, hang up on him, or hide from him again. He was going to confront her face-to-face in her dorm room. He was going to make her listen, and nothing was going to stop him.

Without bothering to knock, Tom burst through the door. "Elizabeth!" he yelled.

The emptiness of the right side of the room hit him a karate chop to the stomach. He actually felt like the breath had been knocked out of him. Grasping the edge of the door to keep himself upright, he took it all in. There were several boxes stacked against the wall but no clothes in the gaping closet. No computer on the bare desktop. No pictures or books on the shelves. No radio. No stuffed animals. No pillows. No Elizabeth.

Slowly his gaze shifted to the other side of the

room. There in the middle of her cluttered bed sat Jessica with her legs curled up under her. Her arms were wrapped around herself as if she could hug away her own misery. With her wild hair and her tear-stained face completely devoid of makeup, Tom hardly recognized her. As she looked at him her eyes were as vacant as Elizabeth's side of the room.

"You're too late," she murmured. "Elizabeth is gone."

Tom's knees turned to rubber. He couldn't seem to catch his breath. He didn't want to break down right here in front of Jessica, but he could no longer hold back the torrent of emotion that had been threatening to flood out for days, weeks . . . as long as Tom could remember.

He sank onto the edge of Elizabeth's bed. With his elbows on his knees he rested his head in his hands as his shoulders began to shake. The release, instead of making him feel better, seemed to unlock the door to all his pent-up emotions. Prefaced with an animal-like howl, he threw himself facedown on the bare, gray striped mattress, covered his head with his hands, and began to sob inconsolably.

Through his own weeping he didn't hear Jessica get up and tiptoe quietly away.

I have to get to Tom before he gets to Elizabeth, Dana told herself as she dashed up the Dickenson Hall stairs. *I can't let them get back together now. Not after all the hard work I've done to keep them apart.*

"Drat it!" she shouted as the heel of her sandal caught in the hem of her long gauzy skirt for the second time. "If I'd known I was going to be chasing around campus playing Mata Hari this morning, I'd have worn jeans and sneakers." She leaned against the green metal handrail and lifted her leg stork style.

But she hadn't known. She'd thought that with Tom safely tucked away in a holding cell at the Sweet Valley precinct, she could lay off tailing him for the day. It'd been a relief to think that Tom was in the hands of Sweet Valley's finest and that by the time they let him go, Elizabeth would be on a plane to Denver and no longer a threat. But she and Scott hadn't reckoned on Nick Fox. Who'd have thought Jessica's cop boyfriend would go down and spring Tom so early?

The minute she'd heard the news that Tom had been released, she'd called Scott and warned him. Then she'd dressed and caught the first bus to campus. It didn't take a Sherlock Holmes to figure out that Elizabeth's dorm was where Tom would head the minute he was freed.

Grabbing the edge of her skirt, she tied it in a big knot above her knees. Then she dashed up the last few steps to the second floor, all the while cursing her lack of a vehicle. "Maybe I should have taken a taxi," she grumbled. "Or borrowed Felicity's car. Stupid buses take *forever!*"

Sliding to a stop in front of room 28, she was surprised to find the door standing wide open. Half of the room looked as if a tornado had passed through it; the other half looked as if it'd been stripped by a school of piranhas. It was totally empty except for Tom sprawled facedown on the battered, bare twin bed.

Elizabeth's, obviously.

His broad shoulders were trembling. He was shaking all over as if he were sick.

Suddenly Dana's breath caught in her throat. She couldn't believe what she was hearing. But as she stepped closer she knew it was true. *He's crying,* she realized. *He's crying his heart out!*

All this for Elizabeth?

Jealousy bubbled up from her stomach, making her feel literally nauseous. She leaned her forehead against the door frame until the feeling subsided.

Tom rose slightly, gasped for air, dropped back to the bed, and resumed crying. Dana had never heard anything like it. *Oh, my poor, poor Tom!* Elizabeth Wakefield deserved to be boiled in oil for hurting him so.

"Tom," she called, hurrying to his side. "Tom." She tapped him lightly on the shoulder.

He looked up. His tear-filled eyes glared at her. "No. Not *you!* Get out of here, Dana."

She shrank back as if he was going to hit her.

"What's the expression of horror for? Do you have your cop friend with you to arrest me for domestic violence again? Just get out of my sight before I really *do* go insane."

She knew Tom would never do anything to hurt her. Her trembling wasn't from fear but from indignant anger at Elizabeth. "Tom, I know you're upset, but I'm here now. Everything is going to be OK. With *her* gone we can—"

"With her gone we can't *anything! I* can't. I don't even want to. I don't care about anything or anyone anymore. Without Elizabeth I'm nothing. Can't you understand that?" Tom closed his eyes and began to rock back and forth on the bed, moaning.

He's losing it, she thought. *And it's all her fault. Elizabeth could have let him down kindly. She could have answered his letter. . . .*

Dana gasped at the thought. Elizabeth couldn't have answered Tom's apology letter because she'd stolen it. Dana's last few weeks with Tom suddenly came into focus as if she were looking through a microscope.

This is all my fault.

Horrified by the realization, her hand floated up to cover her gaping mouth. She stepped backward again and again until the thud of backing into a tall cardboard box stopped her. She stood and stared at Tom.

I've been a complete fool, she told herself. *Here I was judging Scott Sinclair, thinking he didn't know what true love was. And all the time I've been hurting the man I supposedly love.*

"Oh, Tom, I'm so sorry," she whispered behind her hand.

In all her efforts to keep Tom away from

Elizabeth she'd convinced herself that she'd been operating in his best interests, when all along it was her own selfish desires that motivated her. She wanted Tom for herself. She'd become totally possessive, never giving a thought to what Tom might want.

And now she'd ruined his life.

Crossing the room to reach him was like wading through mud. She had to force her feet to take each step, but she needed to make things right.

"Tom," she whispered. She was filled with an almost uncontrollable urge to sink down on the bed beside him and wrap him in her arms. Of course, that was impossible. She couldn't touch him. Any physical contact and she'd be lost again. She had to be strong.

"Are you still here?" he said gruffly.

"I had no idea—"

"You *did*. You *knew* she was leaving today. You've tried your best to get between me and Elizabeth for as long as I've known you!"

"I mean . . . I had no idea how much she still meant to you. I knew you cared about her, but—"

"Cared about her? Care doesn't even *begin* to describe what I feel for Elizabeth. I love her with all my heart."

Dana squeezed her eyes closed. The words couldn't have hurt more if they'd been whips. *Just as I love you,* she thought.

"Just leave me alone, Dana. Go away. Haven't you done enough?"

"Yes," she admitted. "More than enough. I've

186

done way too much." Her voice dropped until it was hardly more than a whisper. "More than you know."

"What?" Tom wiped his face on his sleeve. He was still wearing the same dress shirt he'd had on when the cop stopped him last night. It was sweat stained and wrinkled, and his shirttail hung out. She fought back the impulse to kiss away his tears and straighten his collar.

Please don't hate me, Tom. I love you so much, her heart cried. Knowing everything she'd hoped for between her and Tom was a lost cause, Dana plowed ahead. *Maybe I can at least win back some of his respect by telling him the truth.*

"Tom, before I explain, I . . . I just want you to know that everything I did, I did out of love. I thought we were perfect for each other and you couldn't see it because you were blinded by memories of Elizabeth." She winced slightly as a noise somewhere between a growl and a moan came from Tom's throat, but she held on. "I honestly believed that she was bad for you . . . and I was doing everything for your own good."

"What did you do, Dana. . . ."

"You're right. I *did* try to keep you from seeing Elizabeth, but only because I thought she was hurting you."

"And?"

"And . . . and I also broke your taillights, but I'll pay for them."

"I *knew* it!" He punched the mattress.

187

"But . . . but that's not all."

His eyes narrowed, and he ran a hand through his hair. It stuck up on one side, as if he'd slept on it wrong. "Go on."

"Well . . . you remember that time we had a date and you broke it? You stopped me right out on the parking lot by the music building and . . . and told me we should just be . . . friends . . . well, anyway . . . I was hurt and . . ."

"Spit it out!"

". . . you know that letter you wrote to Elizabeth—"

"Letter!"

"The one where you apologized for the way you acted after . . . something happened with your father. . . ."

Tom's jaw dropped, and he stared at her in disbelief. "How do you know about that letter?"

Dana bent over and busily began to untangle the knot in her skirt. "Uh, well, I sort of found it."

"You found it? Where? On campus somewhere? In the trash? Did Elizabeth throw it away?"

"On her desk . . . at the TV station." Dana hung her head, guilty tears welling in her eyes. "I took it, OK? I was afraid you two would get back together and—"

"You *took* Elizabeth's letter? From her desk? You mean, she never even saw it?" His voice had dropped to a low, dangerous tone. He got up and started to pace. "Dana, do you have any idea what you've done? That paper was more than just my hopes of getting back together with Elizabeth. That letter was an apology for something *unforgivable* that I did. I owed Elizabeth that much, even if we never spoke again."

"I know that now, but . . ."

His face turned redder, and she could see purple veins throbbing on the side of his neck.

"I know you're furious with me," she continued bravely, "and you have every right to be. But I honestly thought—"

"I'm sorry, but I really don't care anymore. Elizabeth is the only thing that matters to me right now." His face became still, emotionless.

Dana sniffed back her tears. "I—I know that n-now," she stammered. "And that's why I'm telling you all this. It was wrong, Tom, so wrong. And . . . and I want you to be happy, so if Elizabeth makes you happy, then . . . Tom, I want you to be with her."

There, she'd said it. She'd finally confessed. And she watched Tom's cool, wooden face for a sign of forgiveness, though she expected none. And as Tom's face burned, his nostrils flaring, his red-rimmed eyes flashing and glistening with fury, she knew she'd never, ever see that sign as long as she lived.

"Hell of a lot of good that does now, Dana! She's *gone!*" Tom roared. "It's too late now."

"It's *not* too late," she insisted, wanting more than anything to do something good for Tom for once in her life. "When Scott heard you were out— er, on your way back to campus, he rushed up here to pick up Elizabeth and take her to the airport early."

Dana decided not to further enrage Tom by admitting that she'd been Scott's informant and spy. "But I know her plane doesn't leave till ten-fifteen," she continued softly. "She's not gone yet. If you went to the airport, you could still catch her."

Tom shook his head furiously. "Right, Dana. Like I should believe you. You've been so honest with me in this relationship!"

"No! Don't say that! I never wanted to hurt you. I just—"

"*Hurt me?* You've done nothing but scheme and lie and con me since we met. How do I know you're not just sending me on some wild-goose chase?"

Dana's eyes filled with tears. "Because I know it's hopeless for you and me now, but . . . I still care enough about you to want you to be happy."

Tom turned away.

"Wait. There's more."

Tom stood towering over her. "More? Wasn't destroying my life enough? What more could you possibly have done, Dana?"

"Not me. Scott. Well . . . I don't actually have any proof." She twisted a strand of hair nervously around her finger. "I just know there's something not quite right about Scott Sinclair. I don't know what; it's just a weird feeling I have. He's just too smooth. Too slick, you know. I don't think he's on the level." Dana stopped fidgeting and looked up into Tom's face. "If you really love Elizabeth, and I know you do . . . then you should get her away

190

from him as soon as possible. I'm serious."

He stared at the ceiling, and his breath became so loud and slow, it frightened her. "You're only saying this to make me more crazy. It's not enough for me to be in pain because I've lost her. Now you want me to believe she's in danger!"

"Not danger, but just . . ." She lifted her shoulders in a shrug.

"But she's gone!" he repeated hopelessly.

"Look," she said, reaching for the pink note on Elizabeth's otherwise bare bulletin board.

"Leave that alone," Tom growled. "You're pretty good at intercepting other people's mail, aren't you?"

Dana winced at his hateful tone, but regardless she pulled the note from the bulletin board and read it.

"See, if you don't believe *me*, here's Elizabeth's flight information: the airline, her flight number, her departure time. . . . Everything's right here." She held the slip of pink paper out to Tom. "Ten-fifteen, see? I told you. There's still time."

He snatched the paper from her fingers and looked at it. Slowly the tense anger on his face ebbed away. The lines around his mouth and eyes softened until he looked like the Tom she'd fallen in love with. She could practically see the love in his eyes, but she knew now that it was a love for Elizabeth. Tom's eyes would never sparkle that way for her.

"Go," she said finally. "If you hurry, maybe you can stop her from making a big mistake."

He didn't speak. He just jumped up and ran

191

out, leaving her alone in the room with her regrets. She kicked a pile of Jessica's clothes across the room. "I do love you, Tom. I even love you enough to let you go," she whispered. Then she sank down onto Elizabeth's empty bed, where it was still warm from Tom's body heat, and cried.

Chapter Eleven

"Oh, Nick. I'm so sorry we fought," Jessica moaned as Nick ran a gentle hand through her hair. She stood cradled in his arms just outside the back door of Dickenson hall, safe and sound. Now that Elizabeth was gone, she needed him more than ever.

After witnessing Tom's misery in her dorm room, running to Nick had been Jessica's first impulse. She was on her way to the Jeep when suddenly Nick appeared, just standing there by his Camaro. Waiting for Tom, he'd said. But to Jessica it had seemed like a miracle—a miracle that seemed to be getting better by the second. Not only was he comforting her about Elizabeth's leaving, but today Nick looked more like his old self. He was wearing jeans and his leather jacket, and his hair was sort of mussed. She nuzzled against his face. It was scratchy, as if he hadn't shaved this morning. And he seemed to have some of his tough-guy attitude back—just a little.

"Want to go get some breakfast?" he asked.

"Um, I guess," Jessica said. "But I'm pretty comfortable right here."

"Well, we can't stay here. I'm parked in a loading zone."

Jessica stiffened. "Is that Nick the policeman talking or Nick the conservative guy?"

"It's Nick the car owner, who can't afford one of those outlandishly expensive campus parking tickets . . . especially now that I don't have a job."

She rolled her eyes and moved away.

He caught her by the wrist and pulled her back into his arms. "Who cares? It's only money."

She was just starting to get comfortable again when she suddenly caught a blur out of the corner of her eye. The blur turned into Tom Watts, who ran around Nick's car and snatched open the passenger-side door.

"Thank goodness you're still here," he yelled. "We have to get to the airport."

Jessica and Nick looked at each other and then at Tom through the open car window.

"Don't stand there gawking at me," he shouted. "Jump in. Both of you. We've got to catch Elizabeth. Her flight leaves at ten-fifteen. We have to hurry."

Suddenly Jessica's depression fell away like broken shackles. She felt alive again. At last *someone* besides her wanted to do something to stop Elizabeth from leaving forever. A huge smile spread across her face. "Well, don't just stand there!" she shouted. "You heard the man. Get in!" She shoved Nick into

194

the car and climbed around him into the backseat. "Let's go, Nick. We have to stop my sister from making the biggest mistake of her life!"

Tom handed her a slip of pink paper. "This is yours. From Elizabeth."

Nick shrugged in confusion. "But—"

"Drive!" Jessica and Tom cried.

As the cab sped along the freeway Elizabeth kept her face turned toward the window so Scott couldn't see that she was crying. She didn't want to upset him any more than he already was. Surely something must have gone very wrong for him this morning to make him act so short-tempered. Ever since he'd picked her up at the dorm, he'd been snarling and griping.

"Hurry it up, man," Scott shouted at the driver.

The cabdriver simply ignored him.

"Hey, you!" Scott rapped his palm on the back of the seat. "You hear me? We've got a plane to catch. Doesn't this heap go any faster?"

"You paying my speeding tickets, kid?"

"No, but I'm paying your fare," Scott retorted. Then under his breath he added, "And you can forget about a tip."

The cabbie seemed to slow the car out of spite. If she hadn't felt so miserable, Elizabeth would have laughed.

She glanced sideways at Scott's tightly clamped jaw and the frown lines around his mouth and eyes.

What's wrong with him? she wondered. *Who is this stranger? Where are the polished, smooth manners that attracted me to him when we first met at WSVU? Where is his gentle sensitivity that finally won me over?*

Elizabeth wanted to believe there was a logical explanation for his sudden transformation. *Maybe he's under too much stress from having to plan this last-minute trip of ours,* she thought. *I guess it's partly my fault. I should have insisted on being a little more helpful.*

"This cab smells like a dirty ashtray," he grumbled.

The cabbie gave no indication that he'd heard Scott's complaint, but it wasn't long before a lit cigar appeared between his teeth. Elizabeth put her hand in front of her nose to block out whatever smoke she could and went back to staring out the window as Scott whined about customer service.

The closer they got to the airport, the denser the traffic. The cabbie had to slow down even more. But even at a snail's pace the airport loomed ahead. Soon they passed a huge green sign that read Departures Only.

Scott squirmed. "You need to get into the right-hand lane up ahead or else you'll get caught in that short-term parking mob," he nagged.

Elizabeth glanced from her window just long enough to catch the cabbie glaring at Scott in his rearview mirror.

The driver merged into the right-hand lane before speaking. "Kid, I make this run about nine times a day. I think I can handle it without your advice."

"Relax, Scott. It's not his fault that traffic is bad," Elizabeth said sympathetically.

"No, it's *yours*," he snapped back. "If you'd been ready to go when I got to the dorm instead of taking so long to say good-bye to your precious sister, we'd have avoided this rush."

Elizabeth blinked and shrank back in surprise. Scott had been crabby the whole trip, but he hadn't come right out and shouted at her.

I don't like this, she thought. *I don't like this at all.*

Jessica groaned as Nick clicked his blinker and moved carefully into the left lane to pass a slower-moving vehicle. He was Nick the conservative guy again.

"Come on, Nick! Turn on the cherry and crank up the sound!" she urged, unsnapping her seat belt and leaning over Nick's right shoulder.

"Jessica, you know I can't use the siren or the dash light. I'm not on the force anymore, remember?"

She made a face. "You're driving like an old gray-haired granny."

"I'm driving like a sane and responsible motorist."

She bounced up and down in the seat. "I can't stand this! Pull over. Let *me* drive!"

"Jessica, get back in the seat and buckle your belt—*now!*" he ordered.

She flopped back in the seat with a huff. "I'm a good driver. Don't you remember that time we

197

were chased by those two creeps in the Caddie who were out to get you?"

"The DeMarco brothers. I'd almost forgotten about them."

"I lost them pretty easily, didn't I?"

Nick mumbled an uh-huh, but instead of looking proud, he seemed pained by the thought. It was only another instance of how he'd changed.

When I saved his butt, he whistled a different tune, Jessica thought. *That day he couldn't say enough nice things about how terrific and special I was.* She crossed her arms and pouted.

"I'm with Jessica. Can't we go a little faster?" Tom asked tensely. "Try the right lane. It seems to be moving faster than this one."

"Yeah. Come on. Go faster, Nick," Jessica urged, leaning forward as far as her seat belt would allow. "We've got to catch Elizabeth."

"Will you two shut up and let me drive? Besides, what good is it going to do if we catch Elizabeth? She's made her choice. Just because you show up waving and screaming isn't going to make her change her plans. She has a future in Denver, and you're both being pretty selfish to—"

"I'm not trying to ruin her future," Tom snapped. "I just have to tell her that I—" His voice cracked. He swallowed before continuing. "Look, what does it matter? Just get me there, OK? I'll take care of the rest."

Jessica's heart went out to Tom. He looked so pathetic. She understood about his rumpled appearance—Nick had already told her about Tom's night in jail. But it wasn't his bad hair and messy shirt that got to her. It was the clenched, miserable expression of hopelessness he wore. Every muscle in his body seemed to be strained to the breaking point. From the tendons making ridges in his neck to his white-knuckled grip on the door handle, he was like a rubber band ready to snap. He really did love Elizabeth. She was sure of it.

"Nick," Jessica said in a stern, no-nonsense voice. "What if it was *me* at the airport?"

Jessica's head was suddenly jerked backward against the seat. The Camaro jumped forward as Nick floored the accelerator. A wide smile broke across her face as Nick finally began to zigzag through traffic like the skilled policeman she'd fallen in love with.

As Elizabeth climbed from the cab the sound of jet engines screaming overhead assaulted her ears. It was certainly more pleasant than Scott's complaining, though. He was being positively unbearable. *What has gotten into him?* Elizabeth wondered. *I've never known him to be so impatient and rude.*

While Scott and the cabdriver got into one last confrontation over getting the bags from the trunk more quickly, Elizabeth watched a harried-looking couple get out of the cab next to them. Between them was a very unhappy little boy.

"I don't wanna go," he whined.

"Come on, Jeffery!" the woman barked, tugging at his arm.

"I don't wanna go on the airplane." He stiffened and began to drag his feet. When that didn't work, he let his legs go as limp as noodles as the couple lugged him into the terminal.

I know how you feel, Jeffery, Elizabeth thought. *I wonder what Scott would do if I started dragging my feet.* The idea appealed to her for some crazy reason, but she knew it was silly. Besides, Scott would probably drag *her* to the plane like a limp noodle too.

"Elizabeth, I could use a little help here."

As she hurried over to Scott a skycap came toward them from the opposite direction. Scott waved him away from their bags. "We've got it," he said. To Elizabeth he muttered, "We don't have time to wait on them."

He picked up her large bag as well as his own and nudged her to precede him.

Why is he insisting on this insanely rushed pace? Elizabeth wondered as they jogged through the busy terminal. Her carry-on bag bounced uncomfortably against her hip with every step. When she paused to switch it to her other shoulder, Scott crashed right into her back.

"Give me a warning when you're going to stop," he grumbled.

She readjusted her bag, and they hurried on through the main lobby. Scott slowed down long

200

enough to read a couple of signs. "This way," he snapped.

"Let's stop in this gift shop for a second," Elizabeth suggested. "I'd like to get a magazine, maybe some—"

"They'll have magazines on the plane," he interrupted, not even slowing down. He hustled her toward the bright buzzing check-in area where Mile High Airlines shared a desk with TWA. The check-in line was relatively short, but Scott snarled anyway.

"Oh! I need to fill out address tags," Elizabeth said as they approached the counter. *That should give me a little more time,* she thought, but then she laughed at herself. *Time for what?*

"I've already taken care of that," Scott informed her, pulling labels from his pocket. "I've got them right here."

When it was their turn, Scott hefted the bags up onto the low counter scales. "Flight three-fourteen to Denver," he said, showing the agent their tickets.

The passenger service agent tapped a few keys on the computer. "We still have several seats available on that flight. As early as you are, you pretty much have your pick. Eleven A and B; twelve A, B, and C; fifteen C and D—"

"Don't bother," Scott interrupted rudely. "Just give us two seats together. It doesn't matter where."

The attendant looked more bored than insulted. "How about these two seats right here?" She tilted a seating chart in Scott's direction so he could see it and pointed out two seats with her green Mile High pen.

"Fine," Scott agreed without a glance in Elizabeth's direction.

Thanks for letting me have my say, Elizabeth thought as the ticket agent began to type their seat assignments into the computer. *Oh, what does it matter where we sit. Every seat on that plane is going to the same place—away from Sweet Valley.*

"It's near the wing," the reservationist said, never breaking her smile. She ripped and shuffled and stapled a few papers with the same official smile and added, "Gate five, concourse C, upper level. Boarding will start fifteen or twenty minutes before the posted flight time. Enjoy your flight, and thank you for choosing Mile High Airlines."

The tall, thin man beside her slapped claim tags on their bags and hefted them onto the conveyor belt.

Elizabeth, watching her bag wobble through a little fringed opening, longed to snatch it back. *Well, that's that,* she thought as it disappeared. It felt somehow final. Too final.

"This way," Scott ordered, tugging on Elizabeth's arm. Once again they were dashing through the airport at breakneck speed.

"Want me to carry that?" he asked as she stopped again to switch shoulders.

"No, I'm fine. But I have to stop at the ladies' room before we get on the plane."

"Elizabeth!" he huffed impatiently. "They'll have a rest room on the plane."

"I know, but as early as we are, it could be a

while before we're able to board. Besides, I hate airplane rest rooms."

He sighed petulantly. "Fine," he said. "But don't dawdle."

Dawdle? she thought angrily. *I'll show him dawdle.*

Humming, she strolled into the ladies' room, stopped in front of the brightly lit vanity, and pulled a cosmetic bag out of her purse. Slowly and carefully she proceeded to reapply powder, mascara, and lipstick. More than she usually wore—but who cared? No one she knew was going to see her anyway. She pulled her hair loose, brushed it, and rebraided it—twice. By that time a line had formed in front of the stalls.

Elizabeth patiently leaned against the cool checkerboard tiles, waiting her turn. When she was the next person in line, a very pregnant woman hurried in with a toddler in tow. Elizabeth smiled politely and let them go ahead of her.

After her turn in the stall Elizabeth carefully washed her hands and dried them under the blower. Watching herself in the mirror, she decided her lipstick needed retouching.

When she finally emerged from the ladies' room, Scott looked livid, but he bit back whatever words he seemed to be dying to say. Grumbling something unintelligible under his breath, he just hurried her toward concourse C.

Elizabeth focused her eyes dead ahead to keep from crashing into anyone at Scott's crazy pace,

203

and the airport beyond Elizabeth's tunnel vision became a blur of sounds. The whine of jet engines was the constant underlying motif, but as they passed lounges, gates, shops, and cafés the surface sounds changed from canned music to PA systems announcing flights to a mumble jumble of voices and back again.

"I'm thirsty," she complained, coming to a sudden halt. "Why don't we stop in this coffee shop and—"

"They'll serve drinks on the plane."

She looked up at the large electronic monitor that flashed flight information. Flight 314 wasn't even listed. They still had plenty of time. What was his big rush?

"Scott—"

"Forget it!"

As they raced toward the gate Elizabeth held back her tears. Why did the long corridor make her feel like she was walking along death row?

Nick pulled in front of the airplane terminal with a squeal of brakes. Tom had the door open and was stepping onto the curb before the Camaro came to a complete stop.

"Tom, wait!" Jessica yelled, but was abruptly yanked back by her seat belt. In the time it took her to unhook it, the automatic doors had already slid open and Tom was rushing inside.

"Wait!" she shouted again, climbing free of the

car. "I have Elizabeth's flight information." She waved the pink note from Elizabeth.

She glanced anxiously at Nick, who motioned for her to go after Tom. But apparently Tom had heard her. He returned and impatiently snatched the pink slip of paper from her hand. Without a word he pivoted around and dashed back toward the airport doors.

"We'll go park in short term and catch up with you later," she called.

But Tom didn't look back.

"Good luck, Tom," she whispered. "For both our sakes."

Elizabeth laid her purse and duffel bag on the X-ray conveyor belt and followed Scott through the metal detector.

She always felt a little bit silly and self-conscious walking through the contraptions. She knew they were for her own protection, but still they seemed slightly excessive. Honestly! Was there really anyone stupid enough to try to walk onto a plane with a six-gun strapped under his shirt?

When the alarm sounded, it was such a surprise, Elizabeth looked around as if to see who'd caused that annoying racket. *Not me,* she thought. But the only other nearby detector was chained off and not being used.

It *had* been her. She'd actually set off the alarm!

"I'm sorry, miss," the security guard said calmly. "I'll have to ask you to go back through, please."

Elizabeth walked gingerly through the gate again. And again the machine beeped loudly.

The security guard handed her a little tray. "I'll have to ask you to empty your pockets, please."

"Oh, great! Now what?" Scott grumbled loudly. He'd already collected the bags that had passed through the X-ray machine and was standing on the other side of the metal detector, fidgeting impatiently.

Elizabeth began to empty her pockets.

Very slowly.

As Tom ran through the terminal's main lobby toward the check-in area people scattered out of his path. From positions of safety they stood gawking and staring.

I know after spending the night in a holding cell I must look scary, Tom thought, *but surely not that bad.* Then he caught sight of his own reflection in a huge window. His unshaven face was swollen from crying. His clothes were rumpled and dirty, and his hair was wild. It was true. He *did* look scary. Still he kept running. Appearance was unimportant at this point. Even when a gray-clad security guard paused, gave him a dirty look, and whispered into a radio, Tom ran on.

I might look crazy, he thought. *But I'm not. In fact, I'm finally sane again. I know what I've got to do.*

Holding her breath, Elizabeth stepped through the metal-detector gate again.

Beeeeeep!

People were lined up behind her now. This was starting to get embarrassing.

"It looks like your leather belt has silver trim, miss. Try removing that," the security guard suggested, patiently holding forward her already growing tray of belongings.

"I can't believe this!" Scott snarled, dropping all the bags in a pile. "Are you going to have her strip right out here? This is ridiculous!"

Beeeeeep!

Chapter
Twelve

"Look out!" Tom yelled as a skycap appeared around the corner pushing an overladen dolly full of luggage. But it was too late. Tom couldn't stop, and neither could the skycap. Tom swerved to keep from crashing headlong into the amazed man, but the luggage cart was right in his path. He crashed into it, sending a virtual avalanche of floral tapestry suitcases sliding across the gleaming airport floor. The skycap spun around off-balance and tripped over a square beauty case. He landed with a thud right on top of an overturned Pullman bag.

A petite, well-dressed woman with her hands in a furry muff began to scream. The muff—which turned out to be a little dog—jumped from her arms and began yipping and yapping.

A young man with baggy pants stopped to help, but the woman turned her wrath on him. "You! Get your hands off my luggage! Guard! Guard! Help!"

she shrieked, swinging her lumpy purse like a weapon.

As the young man noisily tried to convince the woman he wasn't a thief the little dog became one, snatching the skycap's maroon cap and running down the corridor with it.

Nearby a baby started to cry.

Tom struggled to his feet, only to trip on the strap of a garment bag. This sent him reeling into the unlucky skycap, who once again landed seat first atop a suitcase.

Stumbling again to his knees, Tom looked up to see the thick-soled shoes of a security guard thumping along the hallway toward him.

At first Elizabeth had welcomed the delay caused by the persistent metal detector, but now that a long line had formed behind her, she was becoming extremely self-conscious.

The crowd was getting rowdy. People leaned forward to see around others in line before them. "What's the holdup?" she heard someone say rather loudly.

There was a rash of mumbling and explaining and pointing. Elizabeth's cheeks turned red with embarrassment.

"Can't you see she's not a threat?" Scott railed. "We're just college students!"

"Miss, I'll have to ask you to step through once again," the guard said patiently.

"It's your equipment!" Scott insisted. "Your

stupid alarm is malfunctioning, and we've got a plane to catch."

"Sir, please be patient."

Scott tapped his foot and tucked his hair behind his ears. "I'm tired of being patient. I demand you call someone in charge."

The security guard gave him a wilting look and mumbled something into a handheld radio.

"We've got to get to Denver," Scott continued. "If we miss our plane because of this, heads are going to roll. You can bet on it. My father is a close personal friend of Bill Wilson. And just in case you've been living under a rock and don't know who Bill Wilson is, his business conglomerate practically *owns* Mile High Airlines."

Elizabeth glanced at the crowd. A tall, very distinguished-looking man in a business suit frowned at her and tapped his watch impatiently. Desperately wishing she'd never gotten out of bed that morning, she walked through the detector once again.

She cringed when the alarm beeped, even though it should have no longer been a surprise. She glanced apologetically at the line of people behind her, which was getting longer . . . and louder.

Answering the radio page, a second security guard pushed his way through the crowd. He led Elizabeth a couple of steps to one side and began to scan her body with a handheld metal detector.

There was a collective sigh as the crowd behind

Elizabeth began to move slowly but surely through the checkpoint again.

"Well, it looks like our equipment is working all right now," Elizabeth heard the first guard mutter pointedly in Scott's direction.

"Lift your arm, please," the second guard said to Elizabeth.

When the portable detector beeped over her chest, Elizabeth sighed loudly and squeezed her eyes shut.

"You'll have to come with me, miss."

As Elizabeth was led away Scott gathered the bags and followed, grumbling.

Although Tom felt bad about the commotion he'd caused, he couldn't concern himself right now with a bunch of spilled luggage. He didn't have the time.

It'll be OK, Tom told himself as he stumbled away from the overturned luggage. No one seemed to be physically hurt. And the lady with the dust mop dog would probably double the skycap's tip for his troubles. Tom pushed aside his guilt, and after a couple of staggering steps he was once again running full out toward gate 5.

His breath quickened as gigantic orange letters informed him that he'd entered concourse C. *I'm almost there,* he told himself, glancing up at the clock. *I'm actually going to make it!* He felt like a runner at the finish line with no competitors in sight. Daring to smile, he skidded around the corner and dashed down the corridor that led to gates 1 through 12.

Suddenly his smile faded. The corridor was blocked by a huge crowd. Tom jogged to a stop and wormed his way past a few people until he could see what was causing the bottleneck. It seemed there was a problem at one of the metal detectors. Tom craned his neck, but he couldn't see the person behind the security guard. *Some crazy person trying to smuggle a gun aboard,* he thought. He looked at the crowd lined up to wait their turn at security clearance and scowled.

"I don't have time for this," he grumbled angrily.

Not too far away was a metal detector not in use. Despite the thin chain that dangled across it, it beckoned to Tom like an open portal in a science fiction movie. *I can make it,* he thought. *Especially with those guards occupied with the weapon smuggler—or whoever it is that's blocking traffic.* Speeding up, he headed straight for it.

"Hey!" someone shouted. "You can't go through there!"

Watch me, Tom thought. *I wasn't a first-string quarterback for nothing.*

Tom leaped for the gateway. Ducking his head low, he shouldered a guard who stepped in to block his way.

"Stop that guy!" another security officer yelled. A troop of security officers immediately converged on Tom.

Struggling to free his arms from being pinned behind him, Tom argued heatedly, to no avail. As the people waiting to pass through the security check craned their necks and whispered, Tom was hustled away into a nearby security office.

Elizabeth gnawed at a fingernail and stared around the dingy, cramped security office. Everything was a depressing shade of gray: gray file cabinets, gray industrial-grade carpet, gray metal desk piled high with gray clutter. Even the tall, large-boned female security guard standing in front of her seemed like a gray shadow. Elizabeth felt as if all the color had gone out of her life.

"Don't be nervous," the woman said quietly. "All I'm going to do is what we call a pat down. I could have done it out there, but I thought you might prefer a little privacy."

"That's OK," Elizabeth said quietly. She took a deep breath to calm her nerves.

"Are you sure you're all right?" the woman asked. "You look like you're about to cry."

I am, Elizabeth replied silently. *I want to go home.*

She looked into the woman's pale lined face and saw more gray: gray complexion, gray-streaked hair. Even her eyes were gray; perhaps it was due to her gray uniform. The only color that stood out on the guard was her lavender name tag. Elizabeth stared at it to have something to focus her attention on. Captain Hollyberry was stamped on the tag in wide white letters.

"Try to relax," Ms. Hollyberry said. "This is just standard procedure. We can't let someone through

213

simply because they *look* innocent. If we did, every terrorist would recruit a pretty, blond-haired, blue-eyed coed, and then where would we be?"

Elizabeth smiled weakly. As she held her arms at shoulder height she tried to imagine herself at the beach . . . sitting on the SVU quad . . . anywhere except in this dreary office being searched like a common criminal.

The guard was being discreet, but her touch tickled, making Elizabeth shiver. It was embarrassing. She wasn't used to being touched by strangers.

"It's not that we think you look like a serious threat," the woman said as she patted Elizabeth's waist and then down the sides of her legs. "But we have to be very careful nowadays. It's for your own protection."

"I understand," Elizabeth mumbled.

"All sorts of crazy stuff can set off the detectors: keys, nail clippers, belt buckles, metal studs, piercings—you don't have your belly button pierced, do you?"

Ms. Hollyberry chuckled as Elizabeth shook her head no. The guard stopped her pat down and put her hands on her ample hips. "One time we had a guy go through—I don't know how many times—before he told us he had an artificial leg with a metal pin in it."

"What'd you do?"

Ms. Hollyberry laughed loudly. "*I* didn't do anything. But would you believe he pulled the thing off and sent it through the X-ray machine? He was a really good sport about it."

"That seems a little extreme."

214

"Really extreme. I don't think we'll have to yank off any limbs here today. Usually with a woman it's some kind of apparel. Nine times out of ten taking off her costume jewelry does the trick. But since you took yours off and—"

Suddenly Elizabeth remembered something. "Well, there's—" She stopped and looked at the woman sheepishly. Fishing beneath her turtleneck, she pulled a silver chain from around her neck.

"I'm so sorry," she whispered hoarsely. "I put this on this morning under my shirt. I couldn't leave it behind, and I didn't want my . . ." She looked through a slit in the blinds, where Scott paced outside the office door. ". . . my *friend* to see it." She handed the guard the antique-cut steel locket. "It has sentimental value. Someone special gave this to me."

"Not Mr. Impatient out there?"

"No."

Ms. Hollyberry turned the locket over in her hand. "Hmmm. This is made of steel, isn't it?"

Elizabeth nodded.

Ms. Hollyberry ran the hand scanner near it and smiled at the resounding *beep*. Then she ran the scanner the entire length of Elizabeth's body. It remained quiet. *Finally,* Elizabeth thought.

"Looks like a special gift from someone who loves you," Ms. Hollyberry said, handing the locket back to Elizabeth.

"I know it may sound stupid, but . . . I wanted to wear it close to my heart."

Ms. Hollyberry sighed, then smiled. "I know just how you feel. I may not look like any great catch now, but I was in love once too."

"Did he love you back?" Elizabeth asked, reclasping the chain around her neck. The sad smile on Ms. Hollyberry's face struck a nerve.

Elizabeth reached up and unclasped the locket. Why hang on to dreams that could never come true? "Here, you take it," she said. "Keep it or give it to someone who needs a little love."

"No, you keep it." Ms. Hollyberry gently pushed her hand away. "Put it away. Believe me, you'll want it again someday."

Elizabeth shook her head. "No. It's not important anymore." Somewhere in the back of her mind she'd clung to the fantasy that Tom would come and rescue her, but it wasn't going to happen. It was time to accept the facts. This was real life, not a fairy tale. She sighed and dropped the locket on the desk. "If you don't take it, I'm going to leave it."

Ms. Hollyberry picked it up. "Tell you what. I'll hold it for you awhile." She handed Elizabeth a card from her pocket. "That's my pager number. If you decide you want it back, give me a call."

Whatever, Elizabeth thought. *I'll be far away from here by then.*

"Good luck, sweetie," Ms. Hollyberry said.

"Thanks. I have a feeling I'm going to need it," Elizabeth said as she opened the door.

"Because I didn't have time to *wait* for the security check!" Tom yelled for the third or fourth time. He'd answered the same question so many times, he'd lost count. "And I don't have time for this third degree either." He rose slightly from his chair, only to be shoved back down by a security guard tall enough to play professional basketball.

Tom closed his eyes and took a deep breath. *Calm down,* he told himself. *Remember where your temper landed you last night. Explain in a rational manner. The sooner they understand, the sooner they'll let you go.*

"Listen," he began again with as much calmness as he could muster. "I'm sorry I didn't wait to clear the proper security checks. I'm not a criminal or a terrorist. I just need to get to gate five before flight three-fourteen takes off."

"Let's see your boarding pass," the tall security guard asked suspiciously.

"I don't *have* a boarding pass," Tom said, his voice breaking with exasperation. "I'm not flying anywhere. I told you; I'm trying to catch someone before she leaves."

Tom stared hopelessly at the three disbelieving faces surrounding him. The petite, dark-haired female guard seemed his best bet for sympathy. "It's urgent," he added, looking directly into her huge brown eyes.

When she broke away from the huddle, Tom's hopes rose. Maybe she was going to let him go. Maybe . . . but no. She simply moved to the other side of the tiny room and settled behind a desk. With robotic efficiency she began to type information into a computer.

"Your name is Tom Watts," she stated. "And what is your address again, please?"

"Four-eleven Reid Hall," he replied with a disgusted sigh. He was evidently going to have to answer all the same questions again, this time for the computer. "I'm a junior at Sweet Valley University."

"What is your permanent address—your parents' address?"

He gripped the arms of the chair so hard, his wrists cramped. "Reid Hall is my permanent address. I'm twenty-one, legally an adult. My parents are dead." He wasn't about to give them George Conroy's address. He wasn't so sure he still wanted to claim him as a father; from here on out, biology was just a coincidence as far as Tom was concerned.

The guard's fingers clicked across the computer keyboard for a few seconds, and then she picked up the telephone.

While she was occupied with her phone call, the two male guards kept a wary eye on Tom. All the while they kept firing questions at him so rapidly they all ran together.

Who are you trying to catch? . . . Which flight is

218

your friend on? . . . What is the urgent matter? . . . What is this person to you? . . . Have you ever been arrested for a felony? . . . Do you have a criminal record? . . . Do you own a gun?

Tom mechanically answered some of the questions but not all. Most he didn't even hear. He was too busy staring at the stark institutional clock on the wall of the cramped office.

10:02.

Each sweep of the bright red second hand around the black numbers reminded him that time was slipping away.

They're going to keep me from her. Elizabeth is going to leave and I'm going to lose her—forever. All because these stupid people won't listen.

Tom shifted in his chair, and the tall security guard jumped nervously. With the guard's hand on his shoulder Tom leaned forward until he could see the flight display monitor through the room's only window. Under departing flights MHA-314 Denver was now at the top of the list. Beside the flight number the words *Now Boarding* blinked urgently.

"The plane is going to leave any minute," he whined helplessly. "Can't you let me catch up to my friend? Come on. Have a heart. Haven't you ever been in love?" Tom held out his hands, pleading. "You can come with me. Hold a gun on me; I don't care. If you'll just let me talk to Elizabeth, then you can lock me up and I'll answer your questions till doomsday."

219

Chapter Thirteen

"I'm going as fast as I can," Elizabeth snapped at Scott as they skidded around the corner and into gate 5's kelly green waiting area. Most of its benches and hard plastic chairs were now empty. The departing passengers were clumped in front of the open Jetway door, where two airline employees were urging them inside.

"See! Our flight is already boarding," Scott hissed as he steered her into the line.

As Elizabeth stepped into the enclosed Jetway she felt as if she'd just entered the tunnel of doom.

"Here, let me carry that bag." Once again Scott took the duffel from her and hurried her forward. His constant shoving against her back caused her to step on the heels of the woman in front of her.

"Excuse me," Elizabeth whispered. But her embarrassment wasn't complete. Scott, evidently annoyed that the couple couldn't keep up the proper pace, grabbed Elizabeth's hand and dragged her around them. The Jetway was narrow, so their bags and bodies bumped and jostled against each other. Scott seemed totally oblivious to the dirty looks he received.

At the jet's doorway a red-haired, freckle-faced flight attendant smiled politely and welcomed them aboard. After a quick glance at their boarding passes she pointed them toward their seats.

Scott bulldozed Elizabeth down the aisle. Motioning her on to the window seat, he opened the overhead compartment and began stuffing her leather duffel inside.

"Wait," Elizabeth said, ignoring his inconvenienced look. "I want to keep the carry-on bag with me. I can slip it under the seat."

Scott passed Elizabeth's bag to her, then crammed his own bag into the overhead compartment. Elizabeth bent down and stuffed the duffel under the seat in front of her.

"You don't mind my taking the aisle seat, do you?" Scott asked, settling into his seat and reaching for his seat belt. His tone was suddenly more normal than it had been all day. "More leg room."

"No, that's fine. I prefer the window seat anyway."

Normally Elizabeth loved flying. She especially loved watching the city slip away beneath the plane during takeoffs. But today she didn't know if she could stand the sight of Sweet Valley shrinking from sight. How could she watch it disappear, knowing everyone she loved was down there . . . Jessica, her parents, Tom—

How did his name slip in there? she asked herself angrily.

She looked at the midmorning sun glinting off a row of jets lined up to take their turn on a runway. Her stomach fluttered nervously. Soon she'd be high in the air, leaving Sweet Valley for a new life.

I will watch, she vowed silently. *No matter how painful it is, I'll stare out this window and make my final look at Sweet Valley last as long as I can. I'll keep watching until there's nothing left but clouds, and I'll know that part of my life is over.*

Suddenly Scott reached across her and snapped down the shade.

"Why'd you do that?" she asked.

"The sun was in my eyes. As soon as we take off, I plan to sleep."

Good, she thought. *You certainly need a nap.* She hated the thought of listening to his complaining all the way to Denver. With a sigh of annoyance she flopped back in her seat.

Scott was quiet for a minute at most before raising himself slightly in his seat and peering over the seat in front of him. "Why isn't this plane boarding any faster?" he complained, looking at his watch again.

Why don't you take that stupid watch off and hang it from the seat in front of you? Elizabeth thought, biting back a nervous giggle. *You'd save wear and tear on your sleeves that way.*

222

She reached in the pocket of the seat in front of her and pulled out a Mile High flight magazine. Since she hadn't brought a book or magazine with her, she could either read that or the emergency procedure chart. She opened the magazine to the feature article, "How to Enjoy Air Travel with Your Children."

Oh, joy, how interesting, she thought, rolling her eyes. *Well, it might prove helpful since Scott is acting like a two-year-old brat.* But Elizabeth closed the magazine, stuffed it back into the pocket, and glanced at Scott, who was again yanking his sleeve up to check his watch.

"Wonder what we're waiting for?" he grumbled. "I thought we were leaving at ten-fifteen. It's already ten-fourteen, and this plane isn't half full."

"What's the rush?" Elizabeth asked at last. "We're on the plane—with plenty of time to spare, I might add. Relax."

"I know, but if they say ten-fifteen, they should leave at ten-fifteen. There could be another connecting flight somewhere—it could cause a lot of problems for people. This is a really slipshod way to run an airline. You can bet Bill Wilson is going to hear about this."

Elizabeth held out her own watch. "I have ten-ten. Maybe your watch is fast."

"What's the difference? We should be taxiing to the runway, not still be stuck here at the gate."

"I'm sure the pilot knows the schedule," she said. "They're going to take off when conditions are right."

"They seem right to me."

"Well, maybe you should go up there and offer to fly this thing for them."

"Maybe I will."

Elizabeth stared at Scott. His hands were clenched against the arms of the seat. He didn't look as if he was enjoying this trip any more than she was.

What's wrong with this picture? she wondered. *This plane is taking me to my exciting new life. My big adventure. My chance to become a great reporter. And yet I'm perfectly miserable.*

Tom looked from one security guard to another. *I can't take it anymore,* he thought. *They aren't listening to a thing I say. These people aren't human.*

"Sam, I think you'd better look at this," said the officer behind the computer. "It seems our young friend here was arrested last night."

When the short, squat guard who answered to the name of Sam walked toward the desk, the tall guard turned curiously to see what was the matter.

The opportunity was there, and Tom went for it. He jumped up, plowed over the surprised guard, and took off.

"Hey, Watts! Stop!"

"After him!"

"We have a situation in terminal two. Concourse C, near gate three. Station six. We need assistance!"

* * *

"What is your problem?" Elizabeth demanded, giving in to her temper at last. "Why are you acting like you're the travel commando or something? You're making me miserable."

"*Me?*" Scott countered. "*You're* the one who's acting like a kid being carted off to day care for the first time."

"I am not!"

"You most certainly are!"

Scott's blue eyes flashed angrily. "You've done everything in your power to try and miss this flight! Every time I've turned around, there you were setting up some roadblock. You act like you don't even want to leave at all!"

"Well, maybe I don't," Elizabeth admitted hesitantly.

Scott's face turned purple. "You're not being kidnapped, you know. You're the one who decided we should leave early."

"Well, maybe I'm changing my mind!"

"Great. Another example of your immaturity."

"Scott, hush. Everybody is staring at us."

"Talk about ingratitude! After all the plans I've made, this is the thanks I get," he hissed. "You make me sorry I ever wasted my time on you. Do you honestly believe for one moment that you'd have gotten into DCIR if not for me? I'm the one with the connections, or have you conveniently forgotten all about that?"

Elizabeth's fingers instinctively curled into

claw-bearing weapons, but she managed to keep them at her sides. "You may have given me the application and urged me to try, Scott, but *I'm* the one with experience. I got into DCIR on my own merit."

"Dream on."

"Don't talk to me anymore, Scott." She leaned back and closed her eyes.

"I'm sorry, Elizabeth. I guess I am a little cranky today. But don't do this. Yes, you are a good reporter. But together we can be *great*. You can't break up the perfect couple."

"Couple?" Elizabeth said, turning back toward him. "I don't think so. Not after today."

Scott slammed his fist into the back of the seat in front of him. "It's *him*, isn't it? He got to you. I *knew* it! You think you can waltz back to Tom Watts and live happily ever after, don't you?" He leaned back in his seat and ran his hands through his hair. "Don't do this, Liz. Think about all our plans. You and I work together better than you and Watts ever did, and you know it. Just think of the success we had with the country-club story."

"Forget it, Scott. I'm not listening anymore." She turned angrily toward the window and snapped open the shade.

Scott reached across, but she pushed his arm roughly away. "I'll look out the window if I want to!" she snapped.

Her eyes filled with tears as she looked down at the ground. The cargo handlers were driving away in their little cart, pulling a train of empty cars behind them. The whine of the jet's engines seemed to change pitch.

Scott's whine didn't.

"Look at everything I've done for you. If not for me, you'd still be wasting your time fetching coffee at that two-bit, cheesy campus TV station. DCIR is just one step away from the big time. Are you willing to throw all that away now?"

I wish I could, Elizabeth thought. The whine of the jet's engines became a growl, and she could feel the vibration through every inch of her body, but that wasn't what was making her stomach clench. *I honestly wish I could. But unfortunately it's too late to get off this plane now.*

Tom raced toward the gate with three security guards on his tail. Now two more were coming at him from the side. For the second time today he resurrected SVU's number-one quarterback. Wildman Watts took over again as Tom dodged and eluded the two guards out to flank him. Then, ducking his head and holding out his arm, he plowed his way through a line of security guards coming at him in the opposite direction. He broke through, but they all joined the parade of guards chasing him.

With one last-ditch burst of speed Tom leaped

over the rail at gate 5, dashed across the empty waiting area, and flung himself against the large green metal door just as it was closing.

A wide-eyed attendant made a crablike backward scramble for shelter.

"No!" Tom shouted. "I can't be too late. I *can't!*" Although he knew it was hopeless, he slammed his shoulder into the door—again and again and again.

Feeling a guard's hands on his arms, Tom sank to the floor in a defeated heap. Quickly the security guards circled him. Tom felt a knee in his side, a tug on his arms, and the handcuffs snapping around his wrists. But there was really no need for force. Tom was defeated. Nothing mattered anymore.

They pulled him to his feet just as the head of security arrived in a little golf cart.

"What's the problem here?" a tall woman asked.

"Captain," one of the guards said. "This guy has been giving us the slip ever since he ran through security earlier."

"His name is Tom Watts," another guard proclaimed. "And he just got out of jail this morning."

"What's going on here, Tom?" the woman asked, leaning toward him.

Tom didn't answer. He couldn't take his eyes off the locket that dangled from the woman's neck.

Elizabeth kept her face turned toward the window. Her heart was breaking. The engines' roar had deepened. Any minute now the giant jet would be pushed away from the gate and begin its lumbering taxi toward the runway. She closed her eyes.

"Elizabeth!"

The voice sounded far away. Had she fallen asleep and dreamed it? She looked out the window but saw only concrete and a few men in orange coveralls and giant yellow ear covers.

"Elizabeth," someone yelled again. "Don't go!"

She unbuckled her seat belt and struggled to see over the seat in front of her.

Standing at the front of the plane, between Ms. Hollyberry and a flight attendant, stood Tom. His clothes were ragged and dirty, and his hair stuck up like a porcupine's, but she'd never seen a more beautiful sight—or a more welcome one.

Scott's face was livid as he grasped at the tail of Elizabeth's jacket. "Liz. Ignore him."

"Elizabeth!" Tom called again. "I love you. Don't leave me!"

Elizabeth tried to climb past Scott, but his long legs blocked her way. He grabbed her arm. "Don't do this," he warned. "You're throwing away your future. *Our* future. Don't be a fool."

But Elizabeth was way beyond listening to Scott Sinclair. She shook loose his grasp and climbed over his outstretched legs, pulling her purse and carry-on bag behind her. Muttering excuse me's, she hurried down the aisle without a backward glance.

Tom held up her locket. "You forgot this," he said.

Tears swam in Elizabeth's eyes, but for the

first time in ages they were truly tears of joy. Trembling with happiness, she flew into Tom's open arms and began raining kisses over every part of his face while the passengers around them applauded and whistled.

"Oh, Tom . . . I love you too!" she gasped as he wrapped her in an embrace that lifted her feet from the floor. She could feel the wild beating of his heart beneath his shirt.

"Don't ever leave me, Liz," he whispered against her cheek. "Never. I can't live without you."

"I won't, Tom," she replied. "Never again. I promise."

Reminded of the time by a flight attendant, Ms. Hollyberry broke them apart. Wrapped in Tom's arms and escorted by her own security patrol, Elizabeth hurried along the Jetway. It no longer reminded her of the tunnel of doom. This time the Jetway seemed more like the doorway to freedom.

As they slipped through the door into the gate area the PA system overhead boomed, "Final boarding call for flight three-fourteen to Denver . . . leaving gate five . . ."

A puzzled Mile High gate attendant cleared her throat. "Excuse me, miss. Your flight is leaving."

Elizabeth glanced up into the face of the man she loved. "I know. But I'm staying," she said happily.

The crowd that had gathered around them

seemed to disappear from sound and sight as Elizabeth Wakefield lost herself in Tom's passionate welcome home kiss.

Sexy Damon Price has just moved to Sweet Valley, and he's the man of Lila Fowler's dreams. But Damon's quickly turning into the man of Lila's nightmares . . . because he may have killed her in a past life! Can Lila change her deadly fate? Find out in the next Sweet Valley University Thriller Edition, LOVE AND MURDER.

SIGN UP FOR THE
SWEET VALLEY HIGH®
FAN CLUB!

Hey, girls! Get all the gossip on Sweet
Valley High's® most popular teenagers
when you join our fantastic Fan Club!
As a member, you'll get all of this really
cool stuff:

- Membership Card with your own
  personal Fan Club ID number
- A Sweet Valley High® Secret
  Treasure Box
- Sweet Valley High® Stationery
- Official Fan Club Pencil (for secret
  note writing!)
- Three Bookmarks
- A "Members Only" Door Hanger
- Two Skeins of J. & P. Coats® Embroidery
  Floss with flower barrette instruction
  leaflet
- Two editions of *The Oracle* newsletter
- Plus exclusive Sweet Valley High®
  product offers, special savings,
  contests, and much more!

- -

Be the first to find out what Jessica & Elizabeth Wakefield are up to by joining the
Sweet Valley High® Fan Club for the one-year membership fee of only $6.25 each
for U.S. residents, $8.25 for Canadian residents (U.S. currency). Includes shipping
& handling.

Send a check or money order (do not send cash) made payable to "Sweet Valley
High® Fan Club" along with this form to:

SWEET VALLEY HIGH® FAN CLUB, BOX 3919-B, SCHAUMBURG, IL 60168-3919

NAME_____
                              (Please print clearly)

ADDRESS_____

CITY_____ STATE _____ ZIP_____
                                                        (Required)

AGE_____BIRTHDAY_____/_____/_____

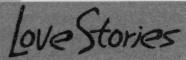